Val,

Pork Chopped to Death

Thanks so
much for all your
help & support ♡

love,
Jodi Rath

Map of Leavensport, Ohio

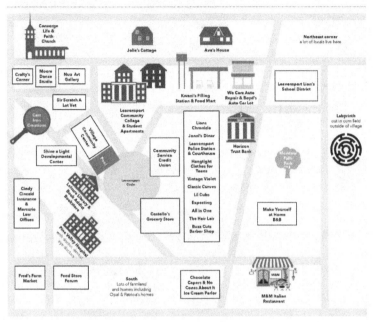

Leavensport, Ohio

Converge Life & Faith Church

Jolie's Cottage

Ava's House

Northeast corner
a lot of locals live here

Crafty's Corner

Moore Dance Studio

Nuu Art Gallery

Sir Scratch A Lot Vet

Kwani's Filling Station & Food Mart

We Care Auto Repair & Boyd's Auto Car Lot

Leavensport Lion's School District

Cast Iron Creations

Leavensport Community College & Student Apartments

Village Community Center

Pool

Shine a Light Developmental Center

Lions Chronicle

Jonni's Diner

Leavensport Police Station & Courthouse

Hangtight Clothes for Teens

Vintage Violet

Classic Curves

Lil Cubs

Expecting

All in One

The Hair Lair

Buzz Cuts Barber Shop

Horizon Trust Bank

Meadow Falls Park

Labyrinth
out in corn field
outside of village

Community Service Credit Union

Leisure Library & Book Addict Bookstore

Leavensport Clubs

Cindy Cincaid Insurance & Mercurio Law Offices

Pine Valley Hospital

Castello's Grocery Store

Make Yourself at Home B&B

Fred's Farm Market

Food Store Forum

South
Lots of farmland and homes including Opal & Patrica's homes

Chocolate Capers & No Cones About It Ice Cream Parlor

M&M Italian Restaurant

One can't build little white picket fences to keep nightmares out. ~Anne Sexton

Pork Chopped to Death

Book 7 in The Cast Iron Skillet Mystery Series

Jodi Rath

Published by MYS ED LLC

PO Box 349, Carroll, OH 43112

jrath@columbus.rr.com

First Printing July 23, 2021

PUBLISHER'S NOTE

This is a work of fiction. Names, characters, places, and incidents either are the product of the author's imagination or are used fictitiously. Any resemblance to actual persons, living or dead, business establishments, events, or locales is entirely coincidental.

The publisher does not have any control over and does not assume any responsibility for author or third-party websites or their content.

The scanning, uploading, and distribution of this book via the internet or any other means without the publisher's permission are illegal and punishable by law. Please purchase only authorized electronic editions and do not participate in or encourage electronic piracy of copyrighted materials. Your support of the authors' rights is appreciated.

https://www.jodirath.com

Cover Design by Karen Phillips at Phillips Covers, www.PhillipsCovers.com

Edited by Rebecca Grubb at Sterling Words, www.sterlingwords.com

Formatted by Merry Bond at Anessa books, http://anessabooks.com

Dedication

This book is dedicated to everyone who has ever felt alienated for one reason or another. This is a strange term to me—alienated—yet I readily admit that many have found me to be odd, weird, or abnormal. It's unpleasant, but I think that most people have felt this way at some point in their lives.

People tend to form groups based on similarities and, in turn, oftentimes those groups alienate others who don't have the same values and opinions that they do. We all do it—it's called being human. But it becomes a moral failure when we become closed-minded and show no level of tolerance for others. People in power often marginalize those who don't measure up to their standards or expectations or those they deem not good enough.

The last several decades of my life has been dedicated to teaching teenagers. The subject I taught was high school English, but I found over time I ended up spending more time teaching lessons on communication and diffusing conflicts that stemmed from these alienations. Because of that, one of the themes that runs through this series is diversity. Many of my previous students, who are now adults, have become my readers and friends. It's important to me that they are ALL represented in this series.

I'm sure you've noticed by now that things are beginning to heat up between the villagers of Leavensport and the city dwellers. Be sure to pay attention to which characters want to bring peace—in our real society, these people are often marginalized or looked down upon when, in reality, they offer so much for all of us to learn from.

While the people in Leavensport and Tri-City will continue to be hard-headed and stubborn, only time will tell if they can learn from past mistakes, make amends, and figure out how to come together, or if they will repeat history and remain divided instead of united.

The Leavensport Crew

Two Protagonists:

Jolie Tucker-Milano-Co-owner of Cast Iron Creations, born in the village, best friend of Ava, granddaughter of Opal, daughter of Patty.

Ava Martinez-Co-owner of Cast Iron Creations, born in the village, best friend of Jolie, girlfriend of Delilah, sister of Lolly, daughter of Sophia and Thiago.

Jolie Tucker's Family:

Grandma Opal-Jolie's grandma, housewife who helped Jolie and Ava start Cast Iron Creations with her cast-iron skillet recipes.

Aunt Fern-Jolie's wacky, unpredictable aunt, sister to Patty, man-hungry.

Patty-Jolie's mom.

Eddie-uncle to Jolie. He, wife Shelly, and their five kids were estranged from the family for decades.

Wylie-uncle to Jolie.

Detective Mick Meiser-Jolie's husband, from Tri-City, transferred career to Leavensport.

Ava Martinez's Family:

Thiago Martinez-Ava's dad; her family lived in Leavensport her entire life but are from Santo Domingo and Theo had to relocate to the

Dominican Republic for work several years ago.

Sophia Martinez-Ava's mom

Lolly Sanchez-Ava's sister.

Theo Sanchez-Lolly's husband

Delilah Sampson-Martinez-Sister of Bradley, village artist, wife of Ava.

Detective Mick Meiser AKA Milano family:

Maria Milano-Mick's sister

Maddox Milano-Mick's dad

Maya Milano-Mick's mom

Imelda-Italian princess who is a love interest from Mick's past.

Leavensport Villagers:

Bradley-Brother of Delilah, village journalist.

Tad and Loreen Sampson-Delilah and Bradley's parents

Chief Teddy Tobias-Police chief of Leavensport and born in the village, best friend of Keith.

Harvey Tobias-Teddy's dad.

Keith-Ex-boyfriend of Jolie, born in the village, best friend of Teddy—now, an officer of Leavensport.

Lydia-Jolie's frenemy, village nurse, best friend of Betsy, born in the village.

Lory-Lydia's mom.

Karl-Lydia's dad.

Betsy-Owns Chocolate Capers, best friend of Lydia, born in the village.

Bobby Zane-new principle of the Leavensport Lions High School—silent partner in Carlos's upcoming new restaurant, Carlos' Hot Tamales.

Nina Sanchez—Mother of Luis and owns a new bakery in town.

Mayor Nalini-mayor of Leavensport, Lahiri is his niece.

Abbey-Mayor Nalini's assistant

Lia-Nestle's ex-wife who is undercover

Devonte-knows who Lia is and protects her

Tom Costello—grocer in Leavensport; dating Grandma Opal

Tabitha-FBI and therapist of Jolie and Mick

Mary-Mirabelle's mom and Carlos new wife

Carlos-Assistant manager at Cast Iron Creations, married to Mary, Mirabelle's stepdad.

Mirabelle and Spy-Young woman with Down Syndrome in her twenties with a seeing-eye dog, Spy.

Ryder Chen-new chef taking over for Carlos at Cast Iron Creations—currently in training.

Tri-City Residents

Jackson Nestle-Unscrupulous political associate of Mayor Cardinal from Tri-City

Caleb and Asher-works for Nestle's Construction Company

Stella-Owns Ralph & Stella's New York Pizza Pie.

Chapter One

Leavensport Lions are LIARS!!!!!

Seeing the graffiti, my shoulders slumped over as I pulled my car into my parking spot for work. Ava, several town members, and I had just cleaned up the walls of the buildings in the art district from the last wave of spray paint.

Normally, summertime in Leavensport, Ohio was hot and humid but beautiful, with lush trees, blue skies, and the sun shining down on our quaint little village. The villagers were typically dressed in tank tops, shorts, with flip-flops and ball caps or floppy sun hats, sunglasses shading their lively, happy-go-lucky eyes as they headed to the center of town to splash in the community pool.

This year, many were still dressed the same, yet a dark cloud seemed to loom over the town with hostile graffiti threatening our tidy little white-picket-fenced world.

I looked at my haggard face in the rearview mirror. I had no make-up on, my jawline was so puffy I had actual jowls, and my ponytail was matted. I hauled my legs—with ankles swollen three times their normal size—out of the car. Then I grunted as I attempted to heave myself into a standing position while weighed down by my stomach, with Phil and Lil, our little punkins, growing inside.

I gave my bump a pep talk. "Come along, you two, and please try to keep the kicking to a minimum today, okay? Mommy's not sure how she will make it another three months with all this kicking and extra weight that I'm lugging around." I rubbed my belly with one hand and put the other on my lower back that was in constant pain now that I'd gained an extra twenty-five pounds. My doc, Dr. La Flesche, instructed me to begin eating an additional six hundred calories a day, seeing that my body was housing fraternal twins.

"Can you BELIEVE they did it AGAIN?" Ava came storming out of the restaurant, hands splayed in the air, eyes bulging, looking at the newest graffiti. "I mean, this is getting ridiculous."

"All of the businesses have cameras set up now, Ava. We'll figure out who is behind the graffiti soon enough."

"It doesn't matter. I already checked our cameras. All of them are covered head to toe in black outfits and masks and gloves and sunglasses. They even waved to the cameras," Ava said through gritted teeth. "The fact they wrote 'Leavensport Lions' makes me think it's teens. Tri-City punks!"

The majority of villagers blamed residents of the nearby city for the graffiti. Tensions had been building between the urbanites and villagers since Ralph, who owned the city's New York-style pizza shop, was poisoned at a festival in our town last fall. Then, over the holiday season, Ava and I found some tunnels leading from the city to Leavensport which seemed to hint at something criminal, or at least nefarious, going on between the two areas. There had been a lot of speculation that the increasing gentrification was causing urban sprawl in our town. There had been a quiet battle building up recently that might finally be boiling over.

"Ava, no one knows for sure who's doing this. I know everyone is assuming it has to do with the recent conflicts between the villagers and our local metropolitans, but it's not good to blame with no proof."

"When did you become an owl?"

"Huh?" I pursed my overly chapped lips, causing them to crack even more.

"Wisdom. Your little pumpkins are making you sensible, oh wise one." Ava brought her hands together and bowed before me, then stood up quickly, moaning and rubbing her preggo belly.

"Punkins," I said without thought.

"What?"

"Not puMpkins but puNkins." I overemphasized the difference, tightening my lips.

"That makes no sense at all," Ava growled.

"Don't get angry. Jeesh! And yes, it does." I crossed my arms. "Mick's grandfather called him punkin when he was little and he's the only man in his family that he admires. So, punkins," I stuck my chin out.

"Sorry, I get overheated quickly lately with my little duckling." Ava rubbed her belly.

"You and I are some pair. Who knew pregnancy was so trying? I feel like moms need to somehow warn future moms of what they are in for," I said, placing a hand on the back of my purple maternity dress and arching my spine further than needed to stretch it out as I walked, making me look like a slow-moving, gigantic, purple weeble wobble. Except, unlike weeble wobbles, I was known to fall down.

"Well, at least part of the graffiti is on the windows, so you and I can use a razor to scrape it off again," Ava grumbled, referring to Delilah, Mick, my entire family, and nurse Lydia yelling at us for not realizing we shouldn't be using solvents while pregnant.

"It will all get figured out over time," I said, humming quietly to myself as I started the coffee pots. Then I walked back to the kitchen to get the Hot Fudge Pudding Cake prepped for the dessert today. Betsy, who ran Chocolate Capers in town, had made a three-tiered-chocolate pudding that I was using in our chocolate cake recipe as part of the cross-selling our village participated in to help out each other's businesses.

"You being so Zen is making me antsy," Ava yelled back before opening up for the day.

Magda came in a few minutes after we opened and said good morning as she got her apron and order pad and hustled toward the front to help Ava.

"Oh, Magda," I yelled before she got through the swinging doors.

"What's up?"

"I just heated up the regulars' breakfasts. Can you carry the to-go boxes up for when they arrive, please?"

"Of course! See, you don't have preggo brain yet!" Magda exclaimed.

I jerked my head back, feeling like I had been slapped in the face. "Have I been forgetful or overly emotional lately?" I tried to keep tears from welling up. I was an emotional person *before* I was pregnant. Now, it was off the charts!

"What, oh NO, Jolie. Ava just jokingly told me to be careful because you had mush brain this morning," Magda started the statement strong, then choked off the last words as she watched the emotions on my face go from sappy sorrowful to irritated. "Sorry," she said before turning to dash up front.

I took a deep Zen breath, breathing in the good and exhaled out Ava's rudeness. Pregnancy made me more emotional than normal, so I'd taken it upon myself to watch some YouTube videos on how Zen practice can help me find peace and calm. But that *was* typical Ava. She and I were the queens of verbal sparring and now that we both were pregnant, I'm sure we'd make an excellent reality TV show. Also, I felt sorry for all the people in our lives and had to tolerate both of us every day while pregnant—like Magda.

I combined the dry ingredients of flour, sugar, cocoa, salt, and baking powder into the bowl, trying to focus on measuring carefully, since I was tripling the recipe to serve the lunch crowd and to be able to take some to our monthly village meeting tonight.

I couldn't believe Carlos was only going to be with us for a few more months. Ava and I needed to start thinking about hiring a new chef who had the potential of becoming an assistant manager. I started mixing in the wet ingredients of milk, butter, and vanilla. I'd been trying to prep more for Carlos because I knew he was working overtime with a new baby at home, overseeing the building of his new Mexican restaurant, Carlos' Hot Tamales, and he was so stressed about leaving us around the time both Ava and I were due with the babies.

I was pretty stressed out about that myself. But Bea Seevers, my family, and other villagers had already promised to help out as much as possible if we hadn't found the right fit for a replacement by then so we would be comfortable leaving the restaurant for a month or so while we figured out how to be mothers.

I finally got to a stopping point and went to the restroom for about the twentieth time that morning. "Hey, I'm going to get the razors from my purse and work on the window a little while there is a lull," I told Ava. She was finishing up with a customer and nodded toward me.

I found the blades and went out front to work on scraping off the spray-painted window. I glanced down at my watch. Just a few more hours before the town meeting tonight. Carlos would shut down early as not many customers would show up anyway. Most villagers attended the monthly meetings at the Community Center. There was always a ton of food at the meetings—pot luck—so we'd all eat well tonight.

I was grinding away, lost in thought, using a soft cloth to wipe off the paint flakes, when a tap on my shoulder sent me jumping straight up in the air. It used to be an easy task—a frightened jump. Now, I felt like I was the Goodyear Blimp crashing from the sky to the ground. I turned around awkwardly to see who it was. Bea.

"Oh dear," Mrs. Seevers said, seeing the discomfort from the jump all over my face. "I'm so sorry. I didn't mean to startle you and the little ones."

Bea Seevers did what everyone else did around me lately, which was to look longingly at my overgrown belly and then hesitantly at me.

"Go ahead," I said, pulling my hands from my bump.

She laid two hands on my stomach and put her head close. "You two are going to be so loved and protected!"

"Oh yes, they literally have an entire village surrounding them in love." I smiled, thinking back to my childhood. There were pros and cons to being born and raised in a small village, and lately, I'd been worried about all the crime associated with the town for decades. Still, in the end, I felt the pros outweighed the cons.

"And protection. You better bet we aren't letting anything happen to Frick and Frack here," Bea said lovingly, referring to my twins.

Everyone in town had funny names made up for the twins and for Ava's little one. "I know. Mick has been adamant about keeping his family away from me the last several months."

"They know you're pregnant, though?" Bea asked.

"I don't think so. After everything went down with Imelda last spring, they took off to Sicily to get her the best defense attorney money could buy. They've reached out by phone to Mick, but he's been ignoring them." I sighed.

"Please tell me that sigh doesn't mean you think they *should* be involved in these children's lives?" Bea tilted her head in a scolding manner.

"I don't know. I mean, I get that they are this huge mafia family—which still freaks me out. But they created Mick. He's amazing, which makes me think they can't be all bad. I can't get him to tell me the entire story with them. All I know is, he walked away from them a long time ago, and I can see the struggle he has when they are around."

"Blood is thicker than water," Bea said.

"I don't agree. My stepdad, Mike, was my true dad. He was the one always there for me as a kid and in my teenage years. When he got cancer, I never left his side." I teared up remembering the relationship I had with him. Right then, a butterfly landed on my shoulder.

Mrs. Seevers' jaw dropped then she immediately slapped her hand over her mouth in excitement and pointed with the other hand.

I slowly turned my head, smiling, as the butterfly flew away. Mike promised he'd always be with me and I felt it and I have seen it literally since he passed on.

"That sort of thing freaks me out." Bea shivered all over.

I rubbed her arm. "The other worlds and spirits are beyond our knowledge. I get it."

Being pregnant the last six months had changed me. I was amazed how quickly I became a mom before I even held them in my arms. And Mick, ugh, I didn't think it was possible to be more in love with him. But yeah, Mrs. Seevers was right— these kids would be protected. He was fierce about that.

"What up, girlfriends?" Ava came bouncing out of the door.

"Someone's in a good mood!" Mrs. Seevers exclaimed.

"I just talked to my family and I *think* I convinced them to hold off their visit for another month or so." Ava's big brown eyes lit up as she clapped her hands together.

I grinned and shook my head. Anyone who didn't know Ava or me would think we hated our families, but nothing could be further from the truth. We were both incredibly headstrong women, and we learned that from the women in our families. We all had a tendency to drive each other batty at times, but doesn't every family?

"How'd you manage that?" I asked.

"I told them not to waste their vacation now. We were waiting to find out the sex of the baby in August so they could come then." Ava's Cheshire cat smile made me giggle.

"Wait, I thought you two didn't want to know the sex?" Mrs. Seevers asked.

"We don't, but Papa wants us to know and he's been hounding me about it since I was nine weeks pregnant."

"She keeps pushing it back and they keep believing her." I shook my head.

"Don't shake that head at me! You are WAY worse than I am with your family," Ava huffed, crossing her arms.

"Hey, it's not my fault that Mick wants to know and I don't. My family is siding with him and it's super annoying! I've given him such a hard time about him and my family ganging up on me that he said he's keeping his shovel in the closet in case he has to defend himself someday from me!"

We all laughed for a moment, then I sighed and shook my head. "I thought he was joking until the other day when I actually found one in there! Oh well, I guess it will be useful next time I'm...digging a hole in the living room?"

Mrs. Seevers let out a loud hoot and slapped her knee. Meanwhile, I noticed figures approaching out of the corner of my eye and turned my head. *Ugh.* Nestle and his henchmen.

"Whoa, ladies, let's get those preggo hormones under control." Jackson Nestle grinned, looking over his shoulder at Caleb and Asher, who both dutifully guffawed.

Ava and my eyes narrowed simultaneously, and I felt the hair on the back of my neck stand at attention. Nestle was, without doubt, a crook involved with the Canadian mafia. Caleb and Asher were his partners in crime, yet no one, including Nestle's ex-wife Lia, could pin anything on him. Ava and I had spent the last few years trying, to no avail.

I started to spout off at them when Mrs. Seevers surprised me by jumping in front of both Ava and me, walking up to Nestle, and jabbing a finger into his chest.

"Listen, gentlemen, these women are worth more than the three of you put together. I hope you aren't planning to dine in this establishment because once these two are out on maternity leave, I won't be so generous as to allow your patronage."

Ava and I were standing behind Bea, but I didn't doubt the bulldog look on her face as Caleb and Asher each took a huge step behind Nestle. Nestle held Mrs. Seevers' stare for a long, awkwardly tense moment, then he turned to Caleb and Asher and said, "I need to head back to the city anyway and I'd much rather give my money to the good folks of Tri-City."

"Yeah, don't forget you have that meeting with Shuttleworth," Caleb said offhandedly as they began moving away.

"You mean your *blood money*," I yelled after him, but they all ignored me and walked off. I noticed that they paused on the other side of the street to talk to an older man in a wrinkled suit. I'd never seen him before.

"Whoa, Mrs. Seevers, who knew you had a killer instinct?" Ava joked, playfully shoving her shoulder.

Mrs. Seevers shook her head, snapping out of her mama bear mode. "Good heavens, ladies. I don't believe I've ever had such a hostile reaction!"

"Well, you are our kids' official Nana. Blood relation or not, you've been a part of our lives since birth." I hugged her, appreciating that Mrs. Seevers was willing to stick up for the babies and Ava and me. "Does anyone know who that Shuttlebutt is?"

Bea let out a heartfelt laugh, her light blue eyes

twinkling. "It's Shuttle*worth*, Jolie, and he's the warden of the prison in Tri-City—Olin Shuttleworth."

Ava and I looked speculatively at each other.

Carlos walked up to us, smiling. "I guess it's slow afternoon, seeing all staff out here!"

"Hey, wow, are you early?" I asked.

"Nope, right on time, as usual." Ava checked her retro eighties Swatch watch for the time.

"A little early, I won't be here long since I'm closing down early for the town meeting tonight," Carlos said, swinging open the door. "I'm going to go in and relieve Magda."

"I guess that's our cue to head home," Ava said.

"I'm going in for a cup of tea and some Hot Fudge Cake," Bea said, giving us both one more hug.

"We'll see you at the town meeting tonight, right?" I asked.

"Oh, you know I'd never miss one." Bea waggled her eyebrows.

"Right, but it feels like it has been ten years and twenty-three days," I whined to Mick as he rubbed my feet before we headed to the town meeting.

"It hasn't. Have I told you lately that you're glowing?" His eyes crinkled with sincerity.

I rolled my eyes.

"What'd I say?"

"Nothing, whenever I whine or get emotional, you always say the same thing—that I'm glowing." I animated the statement with jazz hands around my face and wide eyes. "What am I? A nightlight?"

I attempted to sit up from my reclined position on the couch, but to my utter dismay, my stomach stopped me. I tried to use my head and shoulder strength to help propel me forward, not wanting to take the hand that my overly sweet hubby was holding out because I preferred to pout and let him know *I am woman hear me roar*. It wasn't working well.

Mick patiently reached for me and helped me up to my feet, then kissed me on my nose. "I don't deserve you," I moaned.

"Other way around," he said, then stumbled a bit before getting his balance.

"You okay?"

"Yeah, I think I stood up too fast," he said.

I was always worried another MS flare-up was coming whenever he stumbled. "What'd you mean other way around?"

"You're the one carrying Frick and Frack there, not me."

"You really are a great guy." I reached up to kiss him. Then I kissed him harder. My hands wandered over his shoulders and chest.

"Whoa, we have a meeting to get to." Mick grinned.

"Right. Whew! These hormones are the real

deal."

"I'm hoping they stick around after the kids are born." Mick held the door open for me.

"Nope, it sounds like the kids will kill all those feelings for years to come," I said, playfully patting his cheek with my hand as I walked past him.

"*Noooooooo!*" he wailed in mock horror.

A few minutes later, we were walking into the meeting and ran into Ava and Delilah. Delilah always looked beautiful, but she seemed to be glowing today and had a trendy oversized tie-dye romper on.

"Did you bring the desserts?" I asked, looking at Ava's empty hands.

"I thought you were bringing them?" Ava said.

I saw Mick and Delilah give each other a knowing look that I didn't appreciate. *Those turds.*

"Are you kidding? I told you earlier to bring them and you said you would do it!"

"Nuh-uh, do NOT go blaming me for your preggo brain!" Ava huffed.

"MY preggo brain? You don't even remember me telling you to bring them? You were the last one at Cast Iron Creations!"

Our argument had commenced in front of the door inside the Community Center, and we had stopped walking, effectively blocking the door with our swollen bodies. There was a knock and we snapped our heads around to find a gang of lurkers looking at us nervously through the glass. Then, suddenly, the crowd parted and Carlos proceeded majestically, like a victorious warrior returning from battle, carrying a large bag of what I could only assume was the Hot Fudge Pudding Cake desserts. Throughout the crowd, faces brightened and shoulders relaxed. *Crisis averted!*

Ava and I waddled out of the way as Carlos, the hero of the hour, came barreling inside. "Looks like you two left these at the restaurant. I closed everything down a little earlier since it was dead, and so I could get these to the meeting."

Immediately, Ava and I started to persecute each other verbally again, but Nancy scurried inside with Earl Seevers hot on her tail, which quickly moved the public attention from us to them.

"Now hold on a minute, Nancy. What exactly do you mean by that?" Earl's normally still and steady voice was clamorous and earsplitting.

"Earl, what on earth?" Bea rushed to his side, pulling him away to calm him down.

Nancy, who worked as the receptionist at the police station and also the town gossip, had a face that was as red as a rolling flame of fire.

Even though she drove me batty, as my family had been the object of her notorious gossip-mongering on multiple occasions, I felt bad for her and hurried over to her. "Hey, Nancy, could you please help me take these cakes back to the kitchen? The punkins are really thumping around tonight." I pointed to the humongous round thing that had become my belly.

Nancy smiled appreciatively at the chance to escape and took the warmers from Carlos so he could get to Mary, Mirabelle, and Jorge—the new addition to their family.

"What was that all about?" I couldn't help but ask.

"Ah, you know, Earl has a bit of a history and I should have known better than to bring it up." She pulled the cakes out and carried them out front to put them on the table with all the other food. A moment later, I saw her slip out of the door and assumed she was taking a breather after the scene Earl had made. *Guess I'm not going to find out what that's about.*

I sighed and headed to the table where the food was to load up a plate.

Everyone piled their plates high with barbecue meatballs, pizza, macaroni salad, pies, and cakes and then took their seats, preparing to be talked at while they scarfed down the food—me included.

I glanced over and saw Nancy talking to an older gentleman outside of the door. As the mayor stood up to start the meeting, she pushed him away forcefully and came inside, sitting down.

I walked toward a table, scanning for an empty chair. Teddy came up beside me, also looking for a place to sit. "Who's that guy Nancy was talking to?" I asked.

"That guy? He's the warden at Tri-City Correctional Institution—Warden Shuttleworth. He drove into town today to talk to me about a prisoner." Teddy moved toward Betsy, who had saved him a seat.

Mayor Nalini looked a bit under the weather. He was sweaty and seemed much paler than normal. July in Leavensport, Ohio was typically in the high eighties to ninety-degree range—so sweaty was normal. But we were inside, and they had the air conditioner blasting. Even my sweaty feet were chilly. That was something else pregnancy did to me. I needed to have a climate adjuster like my Honda.

"Let's get started, people." Mayor Nalini pounded his gavel as he loved to do at the beginning and end of each meeting.

"Hey, I don't see anything on the agenda about the graffiti issue," Ava piped up, nearly causing me to spit my meatball out of my mouth.

"Everyone was quiet. You didn't need to scream in my ear!" I hissed as an uneaten chunk of meatball lodged in my trachea, causing me to barely get the words out coherently.

"What? What is with you tonight?"

I gripped the table as my eyes widened and I attempted to cough but wasn't able to. A wave of fear washed over me as the pressure in my stomach combined with the lack of oxygen. I raised my hand to my throat, my eyes wide with alarm.

Ava began slapping my back in a panic.

Grandma Opal snatched an odd device out of her purse as I saw Lydia rushing toward me.

Grandma looked at me. "Trust me, child." She proceeded to put a mask around my nose and mouth, then pull a handle on the front. Immediately, I felt intense suction on my face, then I felt the meatball fly out of my mouth into the contraption.

I took in a sharp breath as tears squirted from my eyes. I sat, stunned, in silence with the rest of the town. After a few seconds, I got the rhythm of my normal breathing back, then felt the blotchy redness move up my neck into my cheeks. I never enjoyed being the center of attention ever since I was a child.

"What is that?" Ava bellowed, bringing all eyes to her.

As much as I hated attention, Ava never minded it and she always found a way to distract whenever the attention was on me.

"The antithrottle!" Grandma Opal held it up as if it was Simba, claiming his new kingdom.

"Oh boy," Lydia said under her breath. She leaned down, looking closely into my eyes. "You don't feel dizzy or anything do you?"

"No, I'm fine."

"If you had lost consciousness, we would have had to take you in to check on the babies." Lydia turned to Grandma Opal and raised her voice. "You shouldn't keep that. It's not approved by doctors and the company is under investigation. That product is potentially dangerous. It could do more harm than good." She reached for the contraption.

Grandma Opal pulled her new toy to one side, protecting it from Lydia's grasp. "What do you mean, young lady?" my grandma interrupted. "This thing just saved my grandchild and my greats."

"Could we continue on with the meeting? I have to be somewhere," Mayor Nalini looked at his watch.

"Why on earth did you schedule a town meeting when you had an appointment?" Grandma asked, setting the antithrottle down and pulling out her chair.

I saw Lydia sneak the contraption under her arm and inch away with it.

"Sorry," I mumbled.

"No need for apologies," the mayor said, smiling at me. "I'm glad you and babies are okay. Now, Ava, yes, the graffiti is not listed. I am handling that situation and I'd ask that no one retaliate or make assumptions about who is doing this." Mayor Nalini started to move to the first topic on the agenda. "The community yard sale is coming up and we need a couple people to be in charge of it. Any volunteers?"

He looked around as many townies stuffed their faces and looked at the table.

"No one wants to take this on? Most of you have things you want to put in the sale. Someone has to be in charge of inventory and setting it up," he scolded.

"Whose idea was it?" Bradley asked.

"My brilliant daughter!" my mom, Patty, said loudly.

I glared at her.

"Ah yes, Jolie and Ava, I believe." The mayor looked at us.

I felt Ava's anger sizzling like a laser beam on the side of my head, causing my feet to go sweaty again.

"Um, right. But look at us." I splayed my hands out at our stomachs, like *nuff said*.

"I seem to recall helping you two solve a little crime spree of theater college kids while pregnant," Lydia piped up.

Ava and I snapped our heads towards her.

"Psst. Grandma, Lydia took your anti-choke-someone device," I said as Grandma whipped her head around, and Lydia looked at her plate with a rascally grin on her face.

"How do we know those city slickers won't show up to paint all over our stuff we're puttin' up for sale?" Zed Zimmerman hollered.

"I just said we aren't going to go blaming anyone at this time," the mayor reprimanded.

Zed, who had a brother, and both were equally large and oftentimes angry, didn't seem to take too kindly to the mayor's comment. He stood as his chair flew back and his chest popped out. "I've had about all I can take from you lately!" Zed pointed toward the mayor, who looked paler than before.

"Okay, we'll do it," I said, wanting to defuse the

situation.

Zed was distracted by my blabbering and got his bearings, grabbing his chair and sitting down, grumbling under his breath. It was odd not to see his brother right next to him as usual.

"Thank you two for volunteering," Mayor Nalini said. "Let's see, if you two can meet with Abbey, she'll get you a list of things to get started then I'll follow up by calling you in a few days."

The mayor looked down at his watch again then at the agenda. Nancy got up from her seat and moved toward the mayor, whispering something to him. He nodded grimly.

"Okay, folks, we need to cut this meeting short. Feel free to stick around and Abbey will lock up later."

With that, he left with Nancy as the rest of us looked around confusedly, then went back to eating.

This had felt like the longest day ever. My feet were killing me and the meeting had me wanting to hibernate until these kiddos were ready to pop. Why did I ever commit to running the community yard sale?

I tried to reach beyond my belly to get my shoes off so I could rub my feet, but I couldn't reach them and breathe at the same time, so I used one foot to shove off one shoe, then the other. I tried to stand too quickly and felt dizzy, taking a moment to let it pass. I took one step toward the kitchen and a leg cramp screamed up at me.

"Swollen ankles, dizziness, leg cramps, constipation, and my gums are so sore I want to scream," I wailed at my little womb demons. "You better be worth all of this. I mean, you best be as cute as can be. I don't even want to know what the third trimester looks like."

I waddled into the kitchen for a glass of milk and saw the dill pickles and grabbed them too. Gulping two pickles in less than thirty seconds and chugging a huge glass of milk, I moaned loudly, rubbing my belly. Just then, as I was pouring another glass of milk, my cell phone rang. I looked at the screen, then eyeballed the pickle jar again before answering.

"Hello," I said while sticking my hand into the sour juice for another green lump of deliciousness.

"Hey, I'm on my way over now," Ava said into the phone.

"Why, what's up?" I crunched.

"Something has happened to Mayor Nalini."

"What?" I set the pickle down, washed my hand, and rubbed Bobbi Jo's little head as she jumped up on the counter.

"He was shot."

Chapter Two

I forced myself to squeeze my swollen feet back into my sandals and headed to our new-to-us Honda CR-V with Ava still on the phone. I still had my Accord, but the belly needed something that I didn't have to squat into or heave to get out of.

"Where are you now?" I asked Ava.

"Near the hospital."

"Just go in and I'll meet you. Make sure Aunt Fern is okay."

"You got it." Ava hung up.

Mick had driven me home then went to his business, M&M's Italian Restaurant, to oversee closing with a new hire, making sure they learned the right way. I wondered if Teddy had reached out to him and I pressed the talk button in the car telling Siri to 'call Mick.'

Calling Lydia.

"What the—" I took a breath, wondering how

Siri thought Mick and Lydia sounded anything alike.

As I went to disconnect, I heard, "What's up, Jolie?"

"Oh, sorry. I told Siri to call Mick and she called you instead."

"That's weird."

"Right?"

"I think you need to do a voice comparison in your system then she'll recognize your voice better."

"How do I do that?"

"I don't know. Don't you have a manual?"

"Yes, but I don't have time to read it."

Silence. I could *feel* Lydia rolling her emerald eyes at me.

"Did you need anything else?" Lydia sighed loudly. I heard Monty, her baby crying in the background.

"Sorry, did I wake him?"

"Yep," she said curtly.

"K—um, I know you need to get him, but I'm trying to reach Mick to see if he knows Mayor Nalini was shot or not."

"WHAT?!?" Lydia shrieked. "Way to bury the lede, Jolie!"

I could tell she went to pick Monty up because his howls were happening directly in my ear. Two of them will do that to me soon. My stomach did a flip-flop as the punkins continued their shenanigans in the womb.

"I'm sorry. I'm a tad preoccupied being pregnant with twins, trying to figure out a new car, driving, and trying to reach my husband!"

"Just maybe focus on going wherever you're going?"

"To the hospital to see what's going on, how he is, and to be with my Aunt Fern."

"Of course, you just focus on getting there in one piece. I'll call Mick."

"Thanks, I appreciate it. Sorry again about waking up Monty."

More silence.

"Hello? Lydia? You still there?"

Okay, some days I was sure our relationship was better and others not so much.

I never liked to pay for valet parking, but tonight, I made an exception.

Getting off the elevator, I saw a crowd of people by the information desk and hustled toward them, looking for Aunt Fern.

Ava grabbed me and pulled me aside before I got to the crowd.

"What's going on?" I asked, taking quick breaths and blinking rapidly.

"Mayor Nalini is still alive, but he was shot in the head and it doesn't look good. They are prepping him for brain surgery."

"Wow, did you find Aunt Fern?"

"She's with him. They can't get her to leave his side." Ava looked down at her hands.

I took a deeper breath in and let it out slowly. I knew my mom would be spastic about more chaos, and my grandma would add to it without meaning to, creating more friction. Aunt Fern may snap under too much pressure from the two of them.

I started toward the information desk to find out where I could find my Aunt Fern, but Ava pulled on my arm.

"There's more, Jolie—" Ava looked down at the ground then met my eyes. "Nancy was with him and she was shot too. But she didn't make it."

My mind was swimming with confusion, and I felt utterly disconcerted. Nancy was dead. Murdered. Someone killed her in cold blood.

"Wait, was she shot? Did they mean for *her* to die or Mayor Nalini or both? They both were shot?" Words continued to tumble out unconsciously. The room started to swim. I felt a thud on my back. A David Lynch nightmarish hallucination took over my mind momentarily.

What was that? "Who are you and what are you doing here?" I demanded.

"QUACK," was both written on a brick wall— was that Cast Iron Creations?—and Donald Duck was quacking at me. He was angry. Very angry.

"Are you mad at me?" I asked, confused.

"QUACK!!!!!!!" Donald screamed, pointing behind me.

I jumped, putting my hands over my ears, turning around into a dark tunnel as a large silver gleam shown down on me. Donald continued quacking, and the noise was unbearable.

I whipped around to shush him, but he was swimming in a large bowl of cherry Jell-O, and his entire body was dripping red. He continued quacking at me in despair.

"I don't understand. What are you trying to tell me?"

I was panicking now.

"Jolie, sweetie—"

I felt a hand on my face, then it went to my hair, petting me like a cat. I swatted it away.

"—it's me, baby. Mick. You're okay now."

"Where—where am I?"

"Jolie, it's Lydia," said a different voice. "You passed out. You're at Pine Valley Hospital in a bed. I've got you hooked up to an IV. You were dehydrated." The world was beginning to swim back into place.

"Why are you yelling at me?" I demanded. "Wait, are they together?" I pointed outside my hospital room door.

"She's confused right now. She'll be fine in a few minutes after the liquids get into her system." As Lydia and Mick talked, I began making out more words and what had happened.

"Weird visions—Donald Duck but red—Jell-O—tunnels." I shook my head, trying to loosen the cobwebs.

"Oh man, you had us freaked out!" Ava barged into the room, slurping a large blue slushie. "Got you one too!" She pulled a Big Gulp from behind her back and held it out to me.

"She may not be ready for that right now—" Lydia started.

I snatched it out of Ava's hand, pushed myself up, and began slurping vigorously.

"Wow, earlier tonight, she couldn't sit up on the couch. Good to know a blue raspberry slushie will do the trick." Mick grinned.

I continued gulping while slugging him in the arm. Then Ava and I both stopped at the same time as our eyes bulged out.

"Brain freeze!" we yelled simultaneously, holding our heads.

"It's so weird you brought this blue slushie. I just saw Donald Duck in a vision, but he turned red in Jell-O—" I started.

"Did you give her some dopey meds?" Ava looked at Lydia.

"A mild relaxant because she was so upset."

Ava nodded, then did a double take. "Wait, you said a Donald Duck dream? I had one of those the other night too!"

"Of course, you did!" My mom came barreling in with another pillow and blanket she stole from a room or from someone. "You both were obsessed with all things Donald when you were kids. Not happy Donald either, oh no, only the grumpy Donald. Doesn't surprise me one bit you both are having weird dreams while you're pregnant."

"Yeah, weird dreams are common. You eat weird foods and your hormones are going nuts when you're pregnant. They could let up or you could keep having them through the third trimester," Lydia said. "My dreams were always about Cruella de Ville when I was pregnant with Monty."

"Of course, it was," I said before guzzling more blue goo, feeling Lydia's gaze rest on me. I grinned.

Lydia giggled. "Nice blue teeth."

I snapped out of my temporary revelry. "Oh my gosh. How is Mayor Nalini? Aunt Fern—where is she? Nancy—" Tears welled up in my eyes.

"We were trying to keep you calm," Ava said. "I didn't know you'd get so worked up before when I told you Nancy was shot."

"You both need to keep your stress under control while pregnant." Lydia pointed at Ava and me. "It's not good for the babies."

"Fernie is with your grandma right now at the chapel in the hospital. There's nothing more we can do other than to keep good thoughts for him. He's in a lengthy surgery and they are doing everything they can for him," my mom said, bending down to kiss my head, then rubbing my belly. "I'm going to go check on them and let them know you are okay. You watch these two!" She pointed at Mick, who saluted her.

"Shut the door, please," I said to Mick.

He obeyed, then came and sat on the bed as Ava pulled up a chair next to us.

"Okay, both Nancy and Fatin Nalini were shot, right?" I asked, putting the Big Gulp on the table tray and lying back.

"Yes, and to answer your earlier question before you passed out—" Ava started.

"Hold on, I just took a solemn oath to keep an eye on you both," Mick said.

"Yeah, you are here watching us?" I gave him the "duh" look, then rolled my eyes at Ava, who was looking at him like he was nuts.

"Anyway, as I was saying, I don't think they know who the shooter wanted—the mayor or Nancy or both," Ava finished.

We both looked expectantly at Mick.

He threw his hands up. "Hey, I can't give you two that information on an ongoing investigation. There's nothing solid right now."

"Why aren't you out there working the case?" I asked.

Mick pursed his lips, lifting his shoulders toward his cheeks. I knew that posture—I did it often with my family and with Ava. I realized he was here because of me.

"I'm fine now. I was having a snack when Ava called earlier and I'm sure the length of this day and so many stressful things happening all got the best of me."

"Not to mention you were freaked out about your Aunt Fern," Ava added.

I nodded my head, curls bouncing around my face. "Everything's okay, babe. I promise. I mean, where am I going to go until Lydia unchains me?" I held up my arm attached to the wires and looked back at the IV. "Please, I'll feel better knowing you're out there, figuring out what's happening."

Mick looked hesitantly at Ava, who gave him a confident smile. He didn't seem convinced as he glanced from her to me. Then he slowly turned and walked out, shaking his head, slumped in defeat.

"Poor guy. He has so many women to manage," Ava said, walking over to shut the door behind him. "OH-MY—" Ava's body froze with the door half-open.

"What? What's going on?" I asked, trying to lean in to get a look, but I could only get so far with the wires.

Ava shut the door and pushed her back to the door.

"WHAT!"

"You're not going to believe who's out there holding hands right now," Ava said.

"Is it Nestle and Lahiri?"

Ava's eyebrows shot up and her jaw dropped. "How could you possibly know that?"

"When I was coming to, I swore I saw them outside the door in each other's arms, but I had had those weird visions and I didn't trust my own eyes."

"Well, you saw what you saw. What's she thinking?"

"I don't know, but don't say anything to her now. She's upset about her uncle."

"I wasn't going to say anything to her," Ava sulked. "Besides, Keith and Marissa are out there with them. They all looked like they double-dated."

I sat up in bed. "Really? Mick never said anything to me about Keith trying to get closer to Nestle that way."

Ava shrugged her shoulders.

At that exact moment, Keith and Marissa walked into the room. Ava and I looked uncomfortable.

"Hey guys," I said, overly casually.

Marissa walked to the bed. "We heard what happened to you. Are you and the babies okay?"

I was shocked by her concern. She and I didn't have a cordial past. "Uh, yeah, we're fine. I'm still getting used to having to eat and drink more than I'm used to. That's all."

Ava was standing behind Marissa, doing a Muppet mimic of her concern. Keith slugged and shushed her while I struggled to keep a straight face.

"Well, we were out with Jackson and Lahiri when she got the news, and when we got here, everything was about *you*."

Touché, Marissa. The manipulative games women play make me insane. I'm so like Meg

Ryan's character in the movie *French Kiss. Match the corresponding face with the corresponding emotion.*

"I mean, she's carrying twins and she took a hard fall," Ava said flatly.

Tabitha appeared just outside the door. "Hey Keith, I'm so happy I caught you here, listen—" She started to reach for Keith's shoulder, not realizing that Marissa was inside the room just out of her line of sight.

I took a sharp inhale of fear that the whole charade was going to go down the drain. Last spring, we'd figured out a mole was positioned in Leavensport—someone who had either had lived here a while or the operation had become multi-generational. Problem was, we didn't know who it was.

We'd figured out some possible suspects and people involved in the crime. Marissa was definitely a person of interest, and Keith was pretending to date her to get information from her. Tabitha, both Mick and my therapist and also an undercover FBI agent, was interested in Keith, as he was in her. They had to keep their romance a secret for now. Fortunately, they were both great at undercover work. I giggled to myself at the double entendre.

"Tabitha, I tried to tell you on the phone that I wasn't interested. This is getting awkward." Keith pushed her hand off his shoulder.

Ava stood frozen, only her eyes darting from Keith to Marissa to Tabitha to me. I sat at attention.

"Oh—uh—yeah. Oh, hi, Marissa," Tabitha's earlier energy was quickly replaced with dismay.

"Hello, Tabitha," Marissa said cheekily, clearly enjoying Tabitha's discomfort.

"I'm sorry. This wasn't—uh—about that. Teddy wanted me to ask you to get some information while you're at the hospital." Tabitha fumbled with her fingers, looking closely at them.

"It's not a problem, sweetie. You have your work." Marissa reached up to kiss him and allowed it to linger a little too long, then grinned at Tabitha and left the room.

Everyone in the room let out a breath.

"I'm sorry I was so rude." Keith took Tabitha's hand after she shut the door and turned around. "I couldn't think of anything else to say."

"Oh, it's fine. I don't give a crap about what she thinks about me." Tabitha waved a hand. Keith looked relieved.

I wish I had that level of confidence and could wave off all the people who drove me batty. I guess that's why she had a degree in forensic psychology, and I didn't.

"With everything that happened tonight, I forgot you were on the double date tonight. How'd it go?" Tabitha asked.

"Wait, when did this happen? How did it happen?" I asked.

"Marissa and Lahiri are friends," explained Keith. "Lahiri started seeing Jackson casually and then Marissa asked if I'd do a double date, so I saw an opportunity. I mean, not much happened before Lahiri got the call about Mayor Nalini."

"Okay, so you're okay?" Tabitha looked at me as Keith turned to make sure I was too.

"I'm fine," I said.

Before I could say more, the two headed out the door.

"I need you to get Lydia," I called after them. "I have to get this stuff off of me so I can check on Aunt Fern and figure out what's going on." I started examining where the needle was inserted into my arm, and the tubes that were hooked to them.

"Just stop! I'll get Lydia!" Ava drug both her hands through her massively thick, dark, natural curls.

I stopped because I could tell I was stressing her out, and I didn't want her to go through what I had earlier.

"You'll be good while I'm gone, right?" Ava tilted her chin, brown eyes narrowed in my direction.

"Scout's honor," I crossed my heart.

"You were never a scout." She shook her head and left.

I laid my head back and took a deep breath in, letting it out slowly. I was starting to feel more normal now. Not necessarily less stressed, but my energy was back up. "I'm sorry, punkins. I'll do better, I promise."

I rubbed my belly and closed my eyes, drifting off to sleep.

A while later, I woke to find Chuck, my biological father, sitting next to my bed.

Chapter Three

"What are YOU doing here?" When I saw my bio dad, those words tumbled out of my mouth without me even realizing it. I regretted it as soon as I saw his eyes brim over with tears.

Chuck and I had an extremely complicated relationship. He left when I was four years old, and that may not have been as difficult for me if he hadn't decided to pop up every three to six years and act like no time had passed and then wonder why I was angry and filled with anxiety to be around him.

The other difficulty was that, as a kid, any time I tried to show anger or disapproval or even honestly describe how I felt, he'd howl like a wounded animal in a way that left deep marks on my psyche. As an older teen, the howling turned into tears and that has continued into my adulthood. This is NOT something I wanted to expose the twins to. My mom tried to get him out of my life, but the court system wasn't in agreement. He was *supposed* to pay child support, but he never did.

Oh yeah—once, when I was seven, visiting him, he tried to take his life. I was the only one at the house with him so I had to run to the neighbor's house—who I didn't know—and beg a stranger to help me. These are just a few of the highlights.

Over time, I'd come to believe he was trying to manipulate me emotionally. I've never fully understood it but had learned to accept it. Now that I was expecting, I knew I'd have to do something about it, but tonight was not the night.

"Sorry." I bit my lip to avoid rolling my eyes.

"You never told Daddy you were pregnant," he said.

Oh man. I was working overtime to keep the disdain out of my voice. I had to or he wouldn't leave. I needed him to leave before Ava got back because she would not try to keep her thoughts to herself. When he called himself 'Daddy,' it made me cringe all over. I instinctively put my arms around my belly as if protecting the twins from his awkwardness.

"Are you okay, baby?" he asked.

"Hello, Chuck." Aunt Fern's voice came from behind me. She quickly advanced across the room to stand over him.

"Aunt Fern, I've been worried sick about you!" I exclaimed.

"I know, I'm sorry I didn't get up here to see you sooner. But you know me. I'll be just fine." She turned to my bio dad and her tired eyes and voice shifted to curtness. "Now, Chuck, not to be rude, but I've had a heck of a day and I need to speak to Jolie privately."

Chuck looked at me as if I should tell her that she was the one who needed to leave. I stared at him indifferently, then said, "I think Ava will be back here in a minute or two."

"I'm going to head out, but I'll check on you tomorrow, okay?" Chuck said, leaning over to kiss my head.

I nodded, but as he left, I couldn't help but sneer, "Yeah, or possibly next year or a few years from now."

Once he was gone I realized how tired Aunt Fern looked. "I'm sorry. How are you? How is the surgery going?"

Aunt Fern plopped in the seat where Chuck had just been. "It's still going. It's going to be a long night. They said it would be hours, and depending on what they found, they may need to close him up and operate again later."

Her hands were shaking. This was one thing I struggled with as an adult. I was used to the women in my family being strong as bulls and always acting so youthful. But lately, I'd seen the strain they go through and started noticing signs of their age on them, and it wasn't pleasant. This would happen to my little ones someday as well.

"I'm so sorry this happened. I don't know what else to say."

"I think I'm still a bit in shock. Nancy is gone. I went to school with her. How is Nancy dead?"

I kept forgetting about Nancy, which made me feel worse. "I—I know. I'm just—" I had no clue what to say. This little village had always felt safe, and I still struggled to believe how many crimes had taken place under our noses for who knows how long.

I had a plan to get all of this figured out and make our village our safe place by the time the twins arrived—but like it does with everything else, life happened. In fact, Ava and I had done little to no more investigating since spring, when we found out we were pregnant. Just then, I heard footsteps in the hall and a figure appeared in the doorway. It was my best friend, Ava.

"Hey, Fernie," Ava said, walking toward her. Aunt Fern rose from the chair for an embrace. "I want to ask how you are but I'm sure everyone is doing that and offering you tea. Right? Everyone seems to think hot tea is the elixir of life when there are problems."

"I mean, it kind of is," I mumbled.

"No one asked you, Smurfette," Ava said, referring to my tongue, which was still blue from the slushie.

"You have a blue tongue too!" I started, then bit off the last word realizing this was inappropriate and childish, considering what was happening.

Aunt Fern laughed heartily. "Oh, you two are just what the doctor ordered! I will never tire of your verbal sparring."

"Well, that's a good thing because no one can be friends with this one," Ava jerked her head in my direction, "without doing some serious bickering. She's impossible."

I smiled and shook my head. Right. *I'm* impossible.

Aunt Fern looked around the room and rubbed her hands together. "Okay, well, I just wanted to check in on you. I hear you're being discharged now. I trust Ava to get you home safely."

"What about you? You need to get some sleep. Why don't you come home with me and we'll come back first thing in the morning?" I offered.

"Nah, I plan to be here when the surgery is over."

"Is mom staying with you?" I asked.

"I told your mom and my mom that I was on my way home." She held a finger to her lips.

"Aunt Fern, someone needs to stay with you," I said. Just then, Lydia popped into the room.

"She'll be fine—I'm here for the night shift, and I have a room set up for her to sleep. I'll take care of her," Lydia said, coming over to my bed to free me from the IV tubes.

"Thank you," I whispered to Lydia. She winked at me.

I slept like a rock and when I awoke, I about fell out of the bed when I saw it was eleven a.m. I shook my head, trying to shake out the cobwebs from the insane day before. I scooted to my black cat slippers and slid my feet into them, waddling down the hall toward the smell of bacon, peppers, and onions.

"Hey, I was going to bring you breakfast in bed," Mick said, piling a generous helping of fried potatoes with peppers and onions in them and lots of bacon onto a plate.

The reality of the day crashed back in on me. I realized I couldn't enjoy this delicious breakfast in leisure. "I was supposed to open the restaurant this morning! We have interviews for a new chef that Carlos wants to be there for because he's going to help train them. I need to get dressed and call Ava and Carlos—"

"Shhhhh." Mick ran around the kitchen island and put his hands on my arms. "You were in the hospital last night. You need to rest. Ava knows that. She and Carlos said you didn't need to come in today."

"What about you? You need to be trying to figure out what's going on in this town. We have two little ones on the way. We need to figure out what is happening!" I was starting to breathe heavily and realized I was wringing my hands.

"Jolie, what's wrong? You're starting to scare me."

"What's *wrong*? The mayor was shot in the head. Nancy's dead. In the last few years, crime has made a pit stop in Leavensport, Ohio, where I was born and raised."

"Crime is everywhere. You know this."

"I do. But I didn't know it's been here all along—my whole life, possibly my mom's entire life. I don't want our kids to have to deal with this!" I sank down into my recliner, leaning back to look at the ceiling.

"No one wants their kids to have to deal with some of the things that happen in this world. We'll take care of them. We'll protect them the best we know how. You have to calm down and focus on taking care of yourself for me, for them, and for you."

I stared at him for a long moment. "Chuck was in my hospital room last night."

"He was? When did he get back?"

"Who knows? It was the same old pattern. Aunt Fern came in and he took off. But I am going to need to have a sit down with him. I don't want him doing to our kids what he did to me."

"Maybe he'll be there for them—" Mick started.

I held up a hand, shaking my head hard. "Please don't. He won't and I'm not taking a chance."

"I get it. I'm trying to figure out how to keep my family in Sicily forever. I don't want them near our kids."

"Wow. Maybe we should change our names and move somewhere?" I shrugged my shoulders, grinning at him.

"And get disguises. You'd look great as a redhead."

"I can see you bald," I teased. "Okay, give me food. I need energy. Don't be angry, but after I eat, I want to go into Cast Iron Creations. I promise I'll take my time and get ready. I want to see if I can be in on some of the interviews."

"How about if I drive you over, then I'll go into work and see what's going on?"

"Deal, but only if you tell me what you know so far."

Mick gazed at me. "Let me warm up our plates and I can share a little with you."

I felt a lot better getting the extra rest and a hearty breakfast. The morning seemed pleasant at first, but threatened to rain as I drove to Cast Iron Creations, hoping to get in on some of the interviews. Lord knows I didn't want to leave the final decisions directly to Ava.

Low-slung, murky clouds sailed across the sky and the wind was starting to pick up. Empty cups, plastic bags, and bits of paper blew along the street, eventually settling against the pavement.

I used my Siri voice control to call my mom, who answered on the first ring.

"You feeling better today?" she asked immediately.

"Yes, slept in—breakfast. Ava and Carlos are

taking over at work. So, I'm resting," I lied, not wanting to argue. "I haven't heard anything yet. How is Mayor Nalini?" I held my breath, waiting for the answer.

"He made it through surgery and he's in a medically induced coma for now. The surgeon is having him monitored around the clock, and they say they will need to do another surgery within the next seventy-two hours."

"Oh man, how did Aunt Fern take it?" I asked.

"She lied to your grandmother and me!" my mom bellowed. "She told us she was going home but she stayed there all night long! I would have stayed with her."

"She didn't want to put anyone out. She's independent and can make her own choices. Mom, I need to go, I'm trying to beat the rain," I said, reaching for the disconnect button. Just as I pushed it, my mom was demanding to know why was I out and where I was. I looked around the CR-V to see if Mick thought to put an umbrella in it by chance.

No umbrella, so I said a silent prayer the rain would hold off until I got into the restaurant.

Typical of my life, I thought to myself as I waddled into the dining room dripping from head to toe. There had been no running from the car to the door, not with the tumbling trapeze twins performing their act in my stomach. Just a slow, soaking shuffle. I stood awkwardly inside the restaurant door, as customers gawked at my soggy misery. Magda gave me a half-wave and turned back to the table she was waiting on.

Carlos and Ava were at a table off to the side near the restrooms for the interviews.

"Jolie, what are you doing here?" Carlos asked, grabbing his jacket from the back of his chair and handing it to me.

"Thanks, but I don't think it'll fit." I looked at his small frame and my large belly.

"No, use it to help you dry off. Please. It's the less I can do. I will run back to the kitchen to grab some dish towels, but use this in the meantime."

"Least you can do," Ava rectified, knowing Carlos had asked us to correct him as he worked to improve his English, "and why are you a drenched rat?"

"Nice," I said, reluctantly, taking Carlos's jacket and wiping my arms, chest, then trying to dry my bare legs from the maternity dress I had on. It wasn't working.

"Here, let me," Ava said, taking the jacket and attempting to bend down to get my swollen legs. She stood back up, shaking her head, then scooted a nearby chair over and sat in it, bending from a sitting position to reach my legs.

"I'm glad bending isn't just hard on me," I said as she rubbed my legs dry.

"It gets worse every day, doesn't it?"

"Ye-ah" I huffed between syllables.

"So, what are you doing here? I told Mick we could take care of everything today."

"I wanted to be here for at least a few interviews." I looked at the clock. "Isn't there supposed to be an interview right now?" I asked.

"Nope, we cancelled the rest this afternoon. We found our guy—" Ava started.

"WHAT?!?"

"No, you'll love him. Honest. He's perfect! Right, Carlos?"

"What's up?" Carlos asked, coming from the kitchen with some towels and handing them to Ava and me.

I wrapped a towel around my dripping hair, and, feeling awkward amongst the customers, I headed back toward the kitchen.

"Ryder! He'll be a great fit here, right?" Ava repeated.

Carlos looked a bit sad, and I turned around to shush Ava.

"Oh, I mean, no one will be able to replace you, Carlos, but—this guy, Ryder—"

"No, I'm sorry. You are right. He is perfect. Do not worry, Jolie. I'm excited about my new restaurant but I'm also going to miss seeing you two and working with you," Carlos said.

"That's called bittersweet," I said, putting a hand on Carlos's arm. "Ava and I feel the exact same way. We are so proud of you and what you've accomplished. You know we will support you in any way we can—" I started walking through the swinging doors to the kitchen then I stopped dead in my tracks.

A very young, very attractive man was using my family's cast iron pans, cooking what looked to be pork chops. He was shorter than me, skinny in a cool, lanky kind of way with a black leather jacket, thick, coal-black James Dean locks that had a bed-head look, full, mauve-colored lips, dark eyes, and a chiseled facial structure. He was striking to look at—he could be a model. Still, no matter how cute he was—he was still in *my* kitchen using *my* family's skillets.

"Who are you and why are you cooking in my kitchen with my family's cast iron pans?" As the words were leaving my mouth, I realized he must be Ryder.

He glanced up, then his eyebrows shot up at the sight of me. "Luotangji!" he said.

"Um, what?" I asked irritably.

"Luotangji," he said again. "A chicken falls in soup." He pointed at my dripping clothes. "That's you. It is the Chinese way of saying...you're soaked!"

Ava started cackling loudly.

I stuttered and gibbered for five or six seconds, grappling with the multilingual dis.

"Dudette, you have a towel wrapped around your head," Ryder added looking from my drenched clothes to the towel on my head, stating the obvious switching to a surfer-dude tone.

"Oh—yeah." I felt a blush rising to my cheeks.

"I'm Ryder Chen. You must be Jolie." He stepped toward me, reaching out to shake my hand.

"Hello, nice to meet you—um, so, are you starting now?" I asked, turning to glare at Ava while not-so-nice thoughts circled around in my mind.

"Oh no, but these two were so kind, I told them I'd come make my Hoisin pork chop special. People in Beijing go nuts," Ryder said, taking a look at my facial expression. "Oh dude, you think I am Barney! Ni ni—I'm no Barney. Don't you worry that curly head of yours," he said.

I was startled. "Oh, I'm so sorry, Ava told me your name was Ryder. Did I call you Barney?" I questioned. I must be losing it more than I thought I was.

Ryder cracked up, hitting his knee hard with his hands. It was a funny, high-pitched laugh.

"You crack me up. I'm gonna have fun with this one!" His eyes grew three times their normal size and he bobbed his head around looking like a long-necked giraffe, then imitating me, "No, I thought you were Ryder."

I looked at Ava and Carlos, who both looked equally confused.

"I'm Ryder. Barney is a flaky surfer. You know—he's such a Barney," Ryder's goofy impression of me turned back to a sexy smile. "Don't worry, I'll teach you all the surfer lingo!"

I shook my head. I didn't know that. I smiled at him and then nodded as if I understood, "Got it,

Ryder, you continue cooking. That smells delish. Ava, can I speak to you for a moment?" I gripped her arm, pushing her through the door behind the counter at the back of the restaurant.

"Have you lost your mind?" I tried to keep my voice steady. "He's insane!"

"SHHHHH!" Ava held a finger to her lips as her eyes and head pointed toward the customers eating. Again, I turned to find half-grins and wide eyes—I realized I still had the towel wrapped around my hair, so I jerked it off my head. "He's different," she insisted. "Plus, did you see those chops? And um—you looked better with the towel on."

"Yes, they do look good and it smells amazing in here—" I started, then stopped when my brain caught up to her insult. I rolled my eyes, deciding to let this one go.

"Not the pork chops—his muscles bulging through that leather jacket and that tight hiney!" Ava started to create cups with her hands but I slapped them.

"Did you hire him because he's good-looking? I mean, you're gay!"

"Yes, I'm aware that I'm gay. It doesn't mean I don't appreciate any gender that is good-looking. Read the room, Jolie—we're in the twenty-first century, you know!"

"No, don't try to shame me. I'm aware and growing and learning and yes, I know I'm privileged." I took a breath, feeling the anxiety swirling through me. "I'm mainly upset that you made a huge decision without consulting me. How hard would it be to call me or wait until the next time you saw me? which would have been sometime *today*!"

Ava repeated my earlier breathing process. "We're trying to make things easier for you, that's all. If he doesn't work out, then we will find a way to let him go. He knows he will have a trial period and that's why it was so important to him to make some food for us. He has a great resume and references and Carlos talked to him while I went to the office to make the calls on his references, which, by the way, were all *glowing*."

"Oh, well, okay then," I still wasn't thrilled, but the intentions were good. The door from the kitchen swung open, and Ryder emerged with three steaming plates in his hands.

"Ah, my beautiful Betties, and my main chef dude—Carlos—I've plated the Chen Hot Hoisin Glazed Pork Chop recipe that comes down from many centuries." Ryder waited as we sat at a table and I noticed customers around us were craning their necks to stare at the fantastic smelling (and looking) pork chops.

"Okay, dude," Ava started. "It's time for one of those lessons you promised in surfer lingo. Betties?"

"Beautiful ladies!" Ryder exclaimed.

He was so childlike and excited with everything he did and said it was impossible not to like him.

His flattery didn't give me the creepy vibe that some guys' compliments do. Maybe I was being too harsh. Plus, he had serious plating skills. The amber glaze was gleaming on the chops and the spices were spread evenly with black sesame seeds and green parsley was sprinkled over the dish for effect.

The three of us cut into the pork and tasted an explosion of flavor. The meat was cooked to perfection, juicy and tender with a combination of salty, sweet, heat, onion, and some subtle smokey notes.

Teddy and Harvey Tobias came through the door, and Harvey immediately came over and peered over my shoulder. "Hey, is that on the specials board today?" he asked. I noticed other customers nodding their heads in agreement.

I thought about struggling to my feet to address the customers, but opted not to. Instead, I shifted in my seat to face them and put on my professional smile and my public-announcement voice. "I'm sorry, not tonight, but everyone—" I gestured toward our new chef, who smiled, "this is Ryder Chen. He will be replacing Carlos when his new Mexican restaurant opens later this fall. Carlos will be working closely with Ryder the next few months to get him trained." I made a broad introduction, then turned back to my food and shoved a huge mouthful of the Asian slaw with the pork in my mouth. *Oh man, even better.*

"Is there onion in this?" Ava asked.

"Yeah, and it tastes like you smoked the meat. Did you bring the pork with you?" I asked, befuddled yet again.

Ryder grinned. "No and no. Ava told me you had some pork out for dinner tonight, so I used some of that with her permission. What you are tasting is this." Ryder pulled a jar of black seeds out of his black leather jacket.

"Sesame seeds?" I asked, using my fork to pick at the black seeds that clung to the pork.

"Nope, Nigella seeds. It's an Indian spice. My ancestors have always mixed seasonings in the recipes we make, and Nigella seeds are one of my favorites. They add a touch of onion flavor and give the meat that hint of being smoked." He smiled and his entire face lit up.

He really was quite charming.

"Well, seems like you might want to share the recipe and put it on the special for tonight," Harvey said. "Cause if you do, I'll be back!"

"I can start tonight if you like." Ryder looked at us.

Carlos looked at Ava and me, nodding. "Oh, I'm happy to work with him and start training and closing." He turned to the new chef. "You will mostly close, and the ladies will need you to fill in on days and sometimes double shifts when they are busy solving crimes." Carlos looked seriously at Ryder.

"Whoa, dudettes, you're crime fighters?

Pregnant Betties fighting crime," Ryder did an impressive Karate chop and kick simultaneously. "I love it!"

"Wow, you make us sound so cool!" I lit up, feeling young again and less like a seven-hundred-pound whale. Maybe it would be really nice having him around.

"But yes," Ryder said, coming back to the original question. "I'm a worker. No worries, I'm ready to dig in."

"I can't imagine how you ended up in Ohio, of all places. Didn't you say you were from Beijing? And you clearly enjoy the beach. Were you a surfer there?" Ava asked.

"Only one good spot in Beijing to surf. The beaches in Wanning, the surfing capital in China. But I lived in California before moving here. But as for living here in Ohio, you have lakes and amusement parks and I will get vacations, right?"

"Oh yes," I said. "We'll do a ninety-day trial period and go from there, but as long as everything works out, we'll get your vacation started after the ninety days."

"Cool, and I can wait—I know you two are due soon. I don't want to take time away from the babies and new mamas."

"The beauty of working here is most of the villagers were born and raised here and we all know one another—someone is always willing to help out," Ava said. "Jolie's family, the Seeverses, you name it."

"I'm going to like this place," Ryder said, loping toward the door. "I'll be back around three if that's good."

We all nodded.

Ryder walked out the door with his right hand, giving the "hang loose" sign as his goodbye.

"Wow, that guy is super cool," Teddy said.

My eyebrows shot up and I grinned. The town sheriff wasn't usually one to say those types of things.

"Who wears a black leather jacket in Ohio in July?" he marveled. "It's like ninety-two degrees out there!"

That was true. And it was cool.

"Hey, you two need to squirty the lime on it— pork and slaw—it's so good!" Carlos exclaimed.

"It's 'squirt the lime,'" I said, feeling guilty. I hated feeling like I was correcting him even though he asked.

"It's okay, Jolie, I want my English to be the best it can be—for Jorge—-when he is learning to talk."

"I get it. You're a really great father, Carlos." I smiled at him while squirting the lime over my plate and watching Ava's reaction after she did the same.

"Oh man, I think my little one loves this dish— she's going insane!" Ava said, rubbing her stomach.

"SHE?" I said too loudly, then dropped my volume. "I mean, 'she?'"

"Oh, we still don't know for sure. I'm positive it's a girl. I mean, it's all female in our house—kitties and all," Ava said before shoving four bites worth of pork and slaw in her mouth.

Carlos laughed out loud. "You two remind me of Mary around this time—what's it called again?"

"Second trimester," I said.

"Right, she was craving all sorts of stuff, and anything she ate was the BEST thing she had ever tasted. Except for chocolate."

"What?" Ava and I said simultaneously with mouths dropped open. Ava's was kind of gross as she hadn't fully swallowed her food yet.

"I know, she loves her chocolate. But not the second tri-mes-ter?"

I nodded at him as Ava gave a thumbs up since she was still chewing from her extremely large bite. I was so happy to see Carlos back to his jovial self again. Last spring, well—it was pretty horrible for Carlos, Mary, and their baby, Jorge. Now that everything was better, he was more like his old self again.

"How has everything been with the restaurant? Anyone bothering you lately?" I couldn't help but bring it up.

"Nope, I'm hoping things will simmer down now that I have a silent partner," Carlos said.

Ava and I looked at each other speculatively.

"Who?" I asked, not caring that I was barging in on his personal business.

"A nice man named Bobby Zane."

Oh boy.

Chapter Four

Since Carlos was training Ryder tonight so he could make his Hoisin Glazed Pork Chops for the townspeople—which I hope they had enough pork because knowing this town, everyone has heard of the dish by now and will be making dinner plans based on it—Ava and I decided to meet back at my place after work so we could do a bit of sleuthing. Ava said she had to stop off at her place to check on the kitties, but I suspected she also wanted a quick smooch from her pretty wife . . .

. . . and probably a snack—probably chocolate.

Wow, I could go for some chocolate right now or some mangos—the orange ones! I don't know why Mick thinks I'm crazy when I say the orange ones are sweeter than the red or yellow ones—he swears it's because it's orange in color and oranges are sweet—but I'm positive my thought process is not that simplistic.

I pulled myself out of the rabbit hole I'd just

went down trailing off about food.

The rain had let up and I was finally dry since Mick brought some clothes to the restaurant earlier to make sure me and the punkins were alright. Although, it was extra humid now, with steam rising from the drying sidewalks like ghosts rising from the dead. I wondered if Ryder still had his leather jacket on.

"Man, you could fry an egg on the sidewalk out there!" Ava said, using the key she made to get in the house moments after I entered. "It feels amazing in here, though."

"I know. I think I'm freezing Mick to death, though. He comes in and puts sweats and a sweatshirt on with socks and goes to bed that way."

"Has he said anything or tried to adjust the temperature without you knowing?" Ava asked.

"Nope, I have noticed a couple of mornings that he must get up and put thermals on under his sweat suit."

"Wow, what a guy! Delilah isn't that *chill*—" Ava used her fingers to air quote the word "chill" to emphasize her double meaning, making me roll my eyes, "—she sneaks the temperature up by one degree every hour or so. Tryin' to be sly."

"And of course, you catch her every time." I grinned.

"You know I do. I think I'm driving her a bit nuts lately." Ava put her hands on her hips.

Shocking, I thought to myself.

Ava either saw something in my expression or read my mind because the next thing she said was accusatory toward my thought process. "I'm positive you're making Mick insane!"

"I think you're a little hangry," I said, reaching for the plate of coconut chocolate candy snacks I'd made a few days ago. I'd forgotten I made them and put them in the fridge to set. I took them out this morning to try them tonight.

"Sorry, this little one is kicking and my breath is always bad even when I brush my teeth seventy times a day!" Ava splayed her arms out, looking about ready to lose it.

"Girl talk—I carry mints with me everywhere now," I admitted.

"Your rack is a freaking national treasure, though!" Ava said, waggling her eyebrows towards my huge lumps.

"Right? Your hair is fuller and more lush than I've ever seen it. I wish that happened to me!"

"I know, but when I dried your legs off earlier, you have no hair on your legs. I've heard that some are lucky enough—how wonderful is that? I still have leg hair, but I don't care. I'm not reaching down there to shave—not with this kickboxing chick inside me," Ava bayed.

"Right, it's not all bad," I started. "Also, we are carrying lives inside us. It's SO weird."

"It really is disturbing, to an extent." Ava looked at me earnestly.

"It's all surreal. It's like I understand I'm pregnant—how could I not know? Yet, I can't imagine taking care of two babies. *I think I'm a little afraid of them*," I whispered the last part.

Ava's eyebrows shot up. "Is this a thing I didn't read about this with second trimester?" She looked terrified.

"What?" I demanded, hands on hips.

"That being pregnant made you literally *insane*?" she whispered back.

"I thought we were having a serious conversation for once! You know, two pregnant women sharing stories." I slapped at her.

"Psssht! You know we don't do that!"

"Okay, you take these—" I shoved the plate of candy snacks at her. "Want some hot decaf tea? I'll make some. You go get our laptops set up and I'll get the tea."

I brought the tea over and all the candies were gone. Ava's expression gave me the impression that she would murder me if I said anything, so I just drank my tea and looked over our I Spy Slides.

"Okay, I'll type a new slide. Mayor Nalini shot in the head—in a coma—needs another surgery currently. Nancy killed. So, first off, who was the target?" I typed while I talked.

"Or were they both targets?" Ava noted as I nodded and added it.

"Also, I still don't know exactly where this happened. I'm going to text Mick," I said, handing the laptop over to Ava as I texted him my question.

Hey babe, you told me a few things about the shooting this morning, but not where it happened. Can you tell me that?

"That's done," I said.

"What'd he say?" Ava asked while pecking away.

"He didn't reply yet," I said as my phone dinged and Ava looked up while nodding to the phone.

Don't you remember, I told you this morning it was at the B&B. You okay?

I clenched my fists and scrunched my eyes shut, growling for what felt like two minutes straight. Then I opened my eyes to Ava typing away, ignoring me.

This annoyed me. "Are you writing a book?"

"Huh, oh—you were having your preggo tantrum, and I have an idea you can talk to Mick about later, and I'll talk to Delilah and we'll get the word spread."

"Oh boy." I shook my head.

"Wait, what did Mick say that made you freak out?"

"Oh, the shooting was at the B&B." I repeated what Mick said. "Supposedly, he told me that this morning but I don't remember it and now I don't know if it's because I have pregnant brain or because he's messing with me!"

"Why would he be messing with you?"

"Because, I mess with him all the time—joking around. I wouldn't blame him for taking advantage of the situation." I pouted.

"I added the B&B and I'm going to note it on our giant slide with the information about the mafias use of the tunnels under Leavensport to Tri-City for smuggling during Prohibition back in the twenties, the information about Bonnie's bones being found in the church basement, and I made a note of all the other things that have happened at the B&B the last few years—not to mention Nestle's group residing there back in the nineties."

"It's a hot spot, for sure," I said. "Hold on, what was your big idea earlier?"

Blinking, Ava tilted her head toward me.

"Before I went off on the B&B tangent—you had a huge idea of something I was supposed to tell Mick later?" This was so like us—all over the map with our thoughts, ideas, and speculations.

"Right! It's been so long since we've looked at this stuff. I realized we have the core group that knows the basics of what is going on—the rise in crime the last few years, the tunnels dating back, a mole in our village. You texted Mick—but the mole in Leavensport is always one step ahead of us. So, I say we come up with a group name, and a code phrase that we can use as an extra layer of secrecy against the mole." Ava sat up taller.

"Wow, that does make sense. Do you think they can get access to our I Spy Slides? Also, do you think the mole is inside our group?" I asked.

"I think either the mole is someone in our group OR we have someone in our group leaking information to the mole." Ava stood and paced a bit, thinking about it all.

"So, they don't have to have access to our slides necessarily if someone is feeding them information," I said more to myself than to Ava.

"Probably would be a good idea to get Bradley and Tabitha involved in the technology part of it and see if they think we need to use burner phones or some kind of a canary trap to figure out who the leak is?" Ava surmised.

"Whoa, being pregnant turns my brain to mush—meanwhile you morph into the next Jessica Fletcher!"

"Brilliance can't be tamed, not even by this one." She pointed to her belly button region. "Okay, you, me, Mick, Delilah know, and Teddy, of course, being the police chief—I'm typing down all the names of the people we've got in our group that we can all trust."

"Right, Harvey—Teddy's dad, and . . . let's see— Keith, he's an officer, Tabitha of course being undercover, Lia since she was married to Nestle in the past—although it still terrifies me to think she's living in disguise right under his nose. I feel like she's gambling with her life." I was referring to Jackson Nestle, the man that all clues seemed to point to when there was trouble—yet no one could pin anything on him.

"Oh, Carlos, Lydia, and Bradley," Ava typed.

"Did I forget anyone?"

"Darrell." I hesitated.

"Darrell—why again? Who trusts him?" Ava asked.

Darrell was Keith's ex-brother-in-law who was shirking his financial duties to his two kids. He was also, in general, an all-around putz.

"Pretty much no one, but Keith was reading him the riot act at the police station when some huge things broke last spring and Darrell—being his—" I started.

"—jackass self—" Ava finished my thought.

"Correct," I continued, "—was eavesdropping. They were ready to throw him in jail for some stupid misdemeanor like trespassing..."

"Imagine that," Ava spit out with disgust.

"...so they had him sign something saying he'd keep quiet or they would go ahead and press those charges. Keith kind of bullied him into confessing."

"Not *really* bullying, though. I mean, Darrell made his bed..." Ava finished again.

"True. Anyway, he's involved now, so we are where we are. At least there is some sort of leverage over him," I said as Ava typed in that information.

We heard someone pull in and I looked at the clock on the cable box. "Mick's home." I smiled.

"Are you two on your I Spy Slides?" Mick asked, walking in. "Delilah told me I'm to keep you both out of trouble. Do NOT get me into trouble with her."

"Why? Cause she scares you?" Ava looked up from typing and grinned at him.

"I'm not an idiot. I'm afraid of all women!"

"Smart man," Ava and I said concurrently. Then, "Jinx!" at once.

Mick rolled his eyes, taking long strides toward me, then bending to kiss me. Then he turned to Ava and kissed the top of her head. "Your hair is amazing!"

"I know, right?" she replied.

Those two were starting to get as bad as me and Ava.

"Hey, thought. We need some sort of secret name for our group." Ava shifted, putting the laptop on the wooden mahogany coffee table Mick had made for us. He'd taken up woodworking as a hobby to help relief the stress of his job.

"Nope," he said, walking into the kitchen for a drink.

"Why?" she demanded.

Mick shrugged his shoulders, popping open a can of beer.

"I talked to my mom today," Mick said, then took a big swig.

"Uh-oh." I looked at Ava, who quickly abandoned her campaign for a code name.

"They want to come back to get their house built. I told her no," he said, sitting next to me.

"Should I leave?" Ava asked, sitting forward to

try and get up unsuccessfully.

"You're family—only leave if you want to," Mick said, and Ava sat back.

"So what did she say when you said no?" Ava asked.

"Silence. That's my mother for you. She wants things the way she wants them and if you don't give her what she wants, then she ignores it and rejects it and makes you feel like crap."

"I can't stand people like that," I said, then realized I may have overstepped. "Sorry."

"No, I agree. It's murky territory because they're my family, but I disagree with pretty much every part of their lifestyle. It's why I ran away and changed my name. I'm telling you, though, they will *not* be a part of our kids' lives."

"Well, you can't stop them from moving here and building their McMansion," I said, referring to the land they had purchased outside of town. The large plot was in the woods leading up to the property line of the Villy Crisis Center, which had always struck me as odd—a snobby, rich mafia family willing to live right next to a homeless shelter.

"True, but I can keep them from being around you and the kids when they get here." He looked tense.

I hated it when he got stressed because it could trigger a flare-up with his MS. The last time that happened, he ended up using a wheelchair, then a cane for what seemed like a lifetime.

"Let's change the subject," I said nervously, looking at Ava.

"Speaking of family, Tad and Loreen have been fueling Delilah's fire about our part-time PI business." Ava waved a hand dismissively.

"Really? I thought you got along with them?" I asked.

"I do. They're great, but with the pregnancy, I think Delilah has been venting to them and now they're worried."

"I get it," I said. "I mean, I kind of get it all. My family worries about me and the kids. So does yours, Ava. Mick and I have had to do therapy to work through how we separate his job from what we do—"

"Not to mention, I work with Tabitha on trying to create boundaries to allow you to make decisions and when to bring things up and how to do so. I worry about you both too." Mick shrugged.

"I worry about you on your job every time you leave," I said.

"Yeah but—" Mick started.

"See, right there—you are going to say 'but I'm not pregnant,'" Ava said. "Delilah does that all the time to me and it's annoying. She doesn't have room to talk." Ava had an odd expression on her face then continued on hurriedly. "I mean, yeah, we are and we get it and we've been taking care of ourselves and the babies but we are also trying to bring them into a safer living arrangement." Ava stuck out her chin.

I pointed to her and nodded.

"Life. It's messy," Mick said.

"Thanks, Confucius." I grinned.

"Okay. Listen." Ava looked eager. "I say our group name is Pudding Up with Relatives. Get it? Pudding—you just made that pudding cake—we're restaurant owners and we love pudding and it's funny and it's a great code that we can incorporate into conversation as a funny between us and if anyone overhears, we just say, 'it's an inside joke' and everyone in the group knows we need to meet!" Ava explained every single thing like a first-grader telling a joke.

"Oh, and everyone in the group should have either a second phone only for group communication OR burner phones!" I squealed. This secret group was exciting!

"Disposables—do people still do that—spies and all?" Ava looked eagerly at Mick.

"Disposables may be overdoing it a bit but as ridiculous as you two make it sound—having some sort of code to use with all involved and a second older phone, like a flip phone, isn't a bad idea," Mick admitted.

Ava had been glaring at him steadily since he called us ridiculous.

"Oh, we forgot to include Gemma and Peggy. Write them down, Ava," I said, thinking of our friends in Tri-City who could provide information about what is going on in the city, since most Tri-City folk seemed to hate us townies lately.

"Okay, I'll be in charge of getting the phones set up for everyone. Print me off a copy of all involved so I don't forget anyone, please," Mick said to Ava, who nodded and clicked "print."

"Ava did we ever make a note about Noah Morrison being the mayor of Tri-City back in 1992?" I remembered when Bradley gave me that information at Chocolate Capers last spring.

Ava skimmed our notes and nodded her head. "It says it here, with a question of whether or not gentrification started then or before that time. Not answered, though, and I don't remember if we asked Gemma and Peggy about it or not."

"I'll text them to double check." I reached for my phone, knowing if I didn't do it now it wouldn't happen.

Bea Seevers' name popped up on my cell as I finished my text to Gemma.

"Hello."

"Jolie, it's Bea," she said in a panicky voice. "I think you may want to get to M&M's."

"What happened?" I asked.

Mick and Ava looked at me.

"It's your uncles and it's not pretty."

Chapter Five

Even though it was only six in the evening, I had very firm plans of being my pajamas with Mick and the cats snuggled up to me in bed right now. Yet, instead, I was in the passenger seat of the CR-V with Mick driving and Ava yacking away in the back seat as we hurried to M&M's Italian restaurant. And we weren't even on our way to eat. No, we were going there to deal with my ridiculous uncles.

"What's wrong with those two? It's been years now! I mean, get over it already," Ava huffed. "But hey, these seats are amazing! Did you two opt for the luxury version? Is so, how come I'm not making that kind of dough?"

"Do you want us to answer some of those questions at some point?" Mick asked, his brown eyes gleaming into the rearview mirror at Ava.

"Yeah, smarty-pants, I do!" Ava gave it right back to him.

"So, yes, it's a luxury with leather seats. Comfy,

right?" I started. "Next, I believe we still make the same amount of money.

"Next question. The uncles are angry. Truthfully, I think Uncle Wylie has a really good reason to hold a grudge. And I get it's not healthy to hold on to your anger, but he had two kids with Shelly that he didn't even know were his until several months ago. After they broke up, she married his brother and then she told Eddie the babies were Wylie's. Wylie had no idea, all those years. The kids have aged—he can't get those years back, Ava. So yeah, that's tough to get past."

"I mean, yeah, it's huge. I'm not denying that. They need to decide if they want to get over it or not—then move on—plus, they're adults. Imagine how messed up the kids are over it—did the kids know?"

"No." I bit my lip. Boy, Ava was going to be a good mom.

Mick tilted his head, glancing at me.

"Right, so bite the bullet and have it out once, figure out what they can handle, then everyone sits down with the kids—talk—and then do it—have a whole family gathering to get it all out in the open if needed," Ava said.

We pulled into the parking lot and Mick drove to the door to let us pregnant types out so we didn't have to walk. We stood and waited while he parked the Honda. Suddenly, a Leavensport police car came barreling in with the siren wailing.

"Oh, good Lord, what have they done?" I said

out loud, trying to get my legs to move faster. Last autumn, at the Leavensport Fall Festival, their argument by the Cast Iron Creations booth had turned into a food fight.

I walked into M&M's and my jaw dropped. Uncle Wylie and Uncle Eddie had torn the restaurant apart—at least the front. Chairs and tables were tipped over, broken glass lay on the floor, no one but Bea and service staff were left, so they'd clearly scared all the customers away.

The two men were circling one another among the wreckage, bellowing insults and swinging at each other. Both of their shirts were torn and they were sweating. Uncle Wylie had a bruise blooming on his cheekbone and Uncle Eddie's lip was bleeding.

Shelly hovered on the outskirts of the squabble, looking horrified, occasionally imploring one or the other of them to "cut it out!"

Mick, Teddy, and Tink pushed past me and Ava to break the two up. After a lot of shoving and grunting, they pushed them out of the front doors to get them out of the restaurant where they could do more damage. Shelly followed, her shoulders slumped, her eyes on the ground.

Ava and I turned to follow them out into the parking lot. "What on earth has gotten into the two of you now?" I demanded. Tink and I exchanged a grim look.

"I wanted to try and make amends with Shelly—and—he—he—" Uncle Wylie started as his normally kind-hearted eyes darkened and he was unable to finish his thought.

"Make AMENDS?!? I came in here and you two were wrapped around each other!" Uncle Eddie shouted. He was short and stout, but like a bull. It was odd he and my grandma butted heads so much as the two had similar body frames—but yeah—both were stubborn as an ox.

"Eddie, we were hugging and I kissed him on the cheek," Shelly said.

"You know, you have nothing to be jealous of— I'm the one who should be jealous. You were always a prick to me because I was younger and more handsome." Uncle Wylie crossed his arms.

"Give me a break, man," Uncle Eddie said. "You're taller. So what? You're tall. And you're only younger by one year."

I was waiting for one or both of them to stick their tongues out at each other.

I saw my mom's car pull in and watched as she erupted from it in a fury. Her cheeks puffed out and a vein was popping out on her forehead as she stormed toward them. Having experienced the business end of that rage, my first reaction was to run and hide. Then I realized I was being ridiculous.

"Um, more like a year and seven days," Uncle Wylie said, sounding a bit like a five-year-old girl, right before lunging back toward Uncle Eddie.

They grappled again as Tink, Mick, and Teddy

grunted, breaking up yet another fight between those bozos. Then, suddenly, they both stopped mid-punch, staring slack-jawed at something behind us.

All of our heads whipped around to where they were looking.

Tom Costello was walking toward M&M's in a nice button-up shirt and tie and some crisp dress slacks. He looked much snappier than he usually did in the old jeans, tee, and ratty old cardigan that he wore to the store daily.

"You better not be dressed for a date with my mom, buddy!" Uncle Eddie pointed a stubby finger in Tom's face.

"Yeah, man, it's bad enough you broke her heart and her trust—now, you're getting all glammed up to try and impress her?" Uncle Wylie joined in.

Wow, it looks like the boys found some common ground after all.

"Whoa, fellas, I'm only here to get some food. I just got back from a meeting in Tri-City. I haven't seen Opal for quite some time." Tom held his hands in the air.

"Yeah, well, you keep it that way!" Tink joined in on the "let's hate Tom" bandwagon.

Tom Costello and my Grandma Opal were supposed to get married alongside Ava and Delilah last December in a double wedding ceremony, but some news about Tom's past surfaced and the bride had second thoughts. So Mick and I had gotten married in their place. Things had been rocky with them ever since.

I felt sorry for Tom. He used to be best buds with Earl Seevers and Harvey Tobias and I'd witnessed an argument between Tom and Harvey, too. It didn't seem like he had many friends lately.

"Sorry, Tom, you can't go in there." Mick stood in front of him before he entered the restaurant.

"What? Now I can't be served here either!" Tom looked devastated.

"It's not you this time," I started. "These two dufuses," I pointed over my shoulder at the uncles, "were fighting and the restaurant is a mess. The staff is cleaning it up now."

"Oh, yeah?" Tom started, as if he wanted to ease some of his own built-up tension toward my uncles, then thought better and stopped.

"What?" The uncles stood side by side, puffing out their chests at Tom.

I mean, I felt bad for Tom, but it was nice for the first time in my life to see my uncles on the same side.

"Nothing." He waved a hand at them dismissively and turned to look helplessly at me. "Last year, when we were still together, your grandma told me about the...situation...with your uncles." He mumbled the last word, then I noticed his attention veer behind me and his eyes suddenly became stormy.

Uncle Eddie looked ready to jump on Tom except he saw the look on Tom's face and again, everyone swung their heads around to see what was going on now.

Grandma Opal was walking toward us in a floral sundress with pretty white sandals, hair set perfectly, made up face—which I hardly ever saw—and a fresh manicure and pedicure in a matching rosy shade. On her arm was none other than Harvey Tobias.

I whipped my head around at Teddy, Harvey's son, who gave me a clueless look.

"What the hell is this?" Tom demanded, pushing Uncle Eddie aside to step in front of Grandma and Harvey.

"Well, it's a date. This lovely young lady did me the honor of saying yes to dinner at one of the finest restaurants in town—" Harvey looked sideways at Ava and me, grinning, then cupped his hand around his mouth and whisper-talked loudly, "—other than your girls' place." He winked at us.

"Don't try to get on the girls' good side. He's just doing that to score points with Opal," Tom flung up his arms in an exasperated gesture and one of his hands whacked Uncle Eddie in the face.

Uh-oh.

"Who are you to hit my brother?" Uncle Wylie shoved Tom.

"I've about had it with the two of you!" Tom put a finger in Uncle Wylie's face before Uncle

Eddie charged Tom, ramming his bald head into Tom's middle, sending him toppling to the ground.

Tom grabbed at Harvey's leg, knocking him down too. The four grown men wrestled around on the asphalt for a few seconds before Tom and Harvey staggered to their feet and started taking jabs at each other. Meanwhile, Uncle Wylie and Uncle Eddie went back to their awkward brother grappling match on the ground. "I was always better than you at wrestling," one of them grunted. "You're a goner now!"

Meanwhile, Tom and Harvey were still at it, their exchange of weird little light jabs turning into them circling while gripping each other's arms and baring their teeth into each other's faces, resembling clumsy, aggressive ballroom dancers.

Grandma Opal looked livid while the rest of us were anywhere from confused to amused to stunned by the chaos taking place in the parking lot of M&M's.

Grandma wedged all four-foot-eight-inches of her rotund self in between Tom and Harvey, yelling out in a high-pitched voice, "EEEEEEEEEOWWWWW, EEEEEEEEEEOWWWWWW!" Then she took a deep breath and did it again. And again.

Ava and I both covered our ears with our hands, as did both uncles, sitting up on the cement. Tom and Harvey both let loose of each other and looked completely stunned.

"MOTHER, what on EARTH are you doing?"

my mom asked, embarrassed.

"You're embarrassed by ME right now?" Grandma's voice cracked a bit from the wailing. She stood, breathing hard, hands on hips looking around at everyone staring at her. "What?"

We all looked one to another then there was nothing left to do but crack up.

I snuck away inside the restaurant. The staff was still hard at work cleaning, but they were making progress.

"Everything okay now?" Bea asked throwing away the last of the broken glass.

"I think so. I'm so sorry, you guys. I'll talk to Mick about some sort of special compensation since you all had to deal with my family and clean all this up." I looked around at the staff.

"Oh honey, no worries. Now, you come here and take a load off and let me get you some ice water. It's still hot out there this evening." Bea led me to a two-top in the corner, then brought a pitcher of water.

"I love my family, but they make me absolutely insane sometimes, Bea." I took a huge drink of the water.

"Family can do that." She smiled. "Your little ones will say the same about you someday."

That wasn't a pleasant thought. I pondered on it a bit more, feeling my emotions well up. I grabbed a breadstick that one of the kids that worked there had brought to the table and chewed on it to get my mind elsewhere, but still felt myself grow teary eyed.

"Oh honey, I didn't mean to upset you." Bea patted my hand. "It's all food for thought. The people we are the closest to are the ones who can make us batty. That's the same for all of us. The love is still there, though—deep down."

"Why didn't you and Earl ever have any kids?" I asked. "You'd make great parents."

Bea got a faraway look in her eyes for what seemed like an eternity, then she snapped back to reality, smiling sweetly at me and patting my hand a few more times before standing up. She leaned over to me, hugging me and kissing me on the cheek, and whispered, "Just know that I plan to always be here for you and your babies. You're like a daughter to me."

"Thanks." I hugged her back, thinking how lucky I was to have good people like her in my life.

The next day, Ava texted that she would run the shop if I'd go question Earl Seevers about his conversation with Nancy at the town meeting.

As I walked up the well-manicured lawn with pink, red, and white peonies blossoming around the sidewalk, I couldn't help but wonder what Mrs. Seevers was thinking of when I asked her about having children. I wondered if there were health issues that kept them from having kids. I hoped I hadn't opened up old wounds for her.

I reached for the doorbell, but it was dangling

by the wires, so instead, I knocked loudly on the screen door, then tried to call, but there was no answer. I turned to leave when I heard something odd inside. *Maybe he is home after all.* I opened the screen door and pounded on the inner door, then pressed my ear against it, listening for footsteps or signs of life.

Was that—a yell? I looked down at the doorbell hanging by the wire again and around the overly elegant front yard. Suddenly, I had a bad feeling. I dialed Mick while jiggling the doorknob. The door was ajar. Another oddity. The door drifted open and I tiptoed inside.

Dang it. I got his voicemail, so I whispered a message telling him I thought something wasn't right at the Seeverses' and I was going inside to take a look. Next, I called Ava at the restaurant.

"Yo," she yelled into the phone.

"I'm at the Seeverses'. Something's wrong," I whispered loudly, walking into the living area and seeing newspapers strewn over the couch and a broken coffee table. In the adjoining dining area, everything had been knocked off of the table and one of the chairs was overturned.

"Aren't they answering? She told me last night they planned to be home today," Ava said.

"I'm inside and it's a mess, and I swore I heard a..." I started listening more carefully. I definitely heard something down the hallway.

"Wait, you're *inside their house*?"

"The door was open! I was worried," I said, inching slowly toward what I thought was the bedroom area.

"Did you call the police, Jolie?" Ava hissed.

"I called Mick and left a voicemail. Ava, I hear someone in a room. What if someone is hurting one of the Seeverses?" I panicked, looking at my belly and rubbing it, then looking at the closed door. The sounds behind it were beginning to resemble torture. "I don't know what to do."

"Leave!" Ava yelled into the phone. "Do NOT put yourself or the babies at risk—walk outside, call the police, flag someone else down—*anything* but being in there alone. Do it, NOW!"

Not realizing she couldn't see me, I nodded in agreement and turned to get out of there when someone grabbed me and my phone flew out of my hand.

"NOOOO, FIRRRREEEEEE!" I yelled, kicking my attacker in the shin, then bringing my elbow down on their back when they doubled over.

"Jolie," the figure groaned, "it's me—Mick." *Oh crap*. The bedroom door swung open.

"What's going on out here?" Bea Seevers emerged, wearing a black, lacy, see-through negligee with black leather stilettos that had silver spikes.

"Oh no!" I gasped, clapping both hands over my mouth. I looked down at my husband who was still wincing on the ground.

"Bea, is everything okay out there?" came Mr. Seevers' voice from inside the bedroom. "Can you please let me loose now?"

This made me question if maybe there was something strange going on after all. It seemed that Mick felt the same, as he got up, limping slightly, into the open doorway.

I walked up behind him to see Mr. Seevers tied to the bed post with a pair of extremely tight black leather briefs on that did not leave anything to the imagination. And...there was a whip in the corner.

"Oh good Lord." I thought I was going to go into labor three months early at the sight. "I am *so—incredibly—sorry*. This is ALL my fault. I will never be able to say sorry enough."

My mind as well as my legs were numb.

"What are you two doing here?" Mrs. Seevers demanded, wrapping an oversized robe around her. She hurriedly threw another robe over Mr. Seevers, then took a dainty knife off of her nightstand and cut his bonds with what looked like well-practiced ease.

"Mick, Jolie, is that you?" Mr. Seevers fumbled for his glasses from the nightstand to get a better look.

Mick stood slack-jawed and did a half-wave at Mr. Seevers.

"Um, I just stopped by to talk to Mr. Seevers and I went to—" I couldn't remember what happened that lead to this. My mind was a blank slate. I looked up at Mick feebly.

He was no help—he had an awkward smile plastered on his face and kept scratching the back of his head and shrugging at me helplessly.

"I mean—your doorbell is hanging on by the wires—" I stated, splaying my hands out like that was justification for all of this.

"I told you to fix that!" Mrs. Seevers pointed a finger at Earl.

"So, I knocked and no one answered. I tried to call but no one answered. I opened the screen door and that's when—" I stopped short of the next phrase.

"When what?" Mick asked.

I glared at him then saw Mr. and Mrs. Seevers stand with arms crossed; Mrs. Seevers foot was tapping impatiently.

"When I heard what I thought was someone yelling—I thought someone was hurting one or both of you...so I...well...I jiggled the doorknob and it opened—"

"You didn't lock the door! Good lord, Earl. Why don't you invite the entire village to our S&M sessions?"

Mr. Seevers bit his lower lip, lowering his chin to the floor, but not before glancing at Mick and giving him a good ol' boys wink.

"I read too much into the situation," I said. "I saw the papers on the floor and the broken coffee table and the—"

"Ahem," interrupted Mick. "Okay, we've done enough damage for one day. I'm going to take my lovely wife into work. Again, we won't say anything to anyone—what you two do behind closed doors is totally—"

"Whoa—hoo-hoo—okay, you two—sexy time!" someone hooted in a loud sassy voice. Everyone turned in surprise. Ava stood in the doorway, grinning from ear to ear.

Please let it end, I thought to myself.

"You called Ava?" Mick asked.

"You need to learn to answer your phone when your wife is expecting twins!" Ava jutted her chin out at him. "I'm here to make sure she's okay. We got disconnected and she didn't pick up when I kept calling."

"Who's at the restaurant now? Magda and Carlos won't be in for another hour," I said, checking the time on my cell.

"I told everyone there was an emergency at the Seeverses' and boxed up their food and put the closed sign up. There's been too many bad things happening lately. I wasn't risking you not listening to me when I told you to get out of here!"

"I tried, but Mick scared the bejeezus out of me," I said through gritted teeth.

"Oh, so now it's my fault!" Mick threw up his hands.

"Kids, I don't really care whose responsibility it is—seems like the whole town will be wondering what went on with us today." Bea scowled at Earl as if this was entirely his fault.

"Nah, seriously, if anyone asks you what happened, just answer with one word." Ava looked at all of us.

"What's that?" Mrs. Seevers huffed.

"Jolie."

Nice.

"I want to run to the hospital to check on Mayor Nalini and Aunt Fern," I said to Mick and Ava as we walked toward our cars.

I noticed a parade of villagers walking and driving slowly past the Seeverses' house.

"These people wouldn't happen to have been the lunch rush, would they?" I pointed to the parade.

"Um, probably," Ava mumbled and we all waved to them and as some of them gave us concerned looks, the three of us gave them thumbs up signs to let them know all was well with the Seeverses.

"They're okay," Lydia yelled out from her Toyota RAV4. Being a nurse, she probably felt it was her duty to make sure there was no medical issues. Who knew what kind of rumors were being spread about the Seeverses?

"They're better than okay, if you know what I mean." Ava waggled her eyebrows. "Jolie just overreacted—as usual," Ava rolled her eyes.

"Nothing to see here folks—it's just Jolie and her antics!"

I hit Ava in the arm.

"Ow, what—I'm not lying to anyone!"

She had a point.

"My life used to be boring," Mick said, seeing Teddy and Keith approaching in the squad car and waving them off.

Keith and Teddy saw Ava and me as they drove by, then shook their heads and cracked up. Maybe I was more of an issue than even I realized.

"Okay, I'm done being the village dunce for the day," I grumped. "Ava, you can head back to open back up—do NOT tell anyone what you saw." I pointed at her nose. I leaned up to kiss Mick, whom I caught sending Ava a look that clearly said *don't rock the boat with her right now*, so instead she just quietly mumbled something while getting into her car.

I headed southwest to the hospital in the CR-V. Counting Crows had been blaring from the stereo so I turned it off completely to work on my breathing exercises. Not only was I working on my Zen practice, but I'd been reading up on what to expect with Lamaze classes Ava and I would be taking in another month or so. As I took deep breaths, I looked around at the sun beating down, causing my windows to fog slightly from the humidity. I purposefully drove past the Leavensport pool and felt a tinge of jealousy, seeing other women my age in their bikinis, wondering if

I'd ever see even a one piece again.

I pulled into valet parking for the second time, feeling a smidge guilty for paying for it twice within a week, but then realizing I'd seen and been through enough today to earn a little break. No one was there. Okay—I waited about five minutes, thinking they'd be back soon, all the while glancing around for a sign saying they were at lunch or on break or something, but saw nothing.

"Great." I pulled into the garage, pushing the button for a parking ticket and hoping I could find a spot near the elevator.

No such luck. I had to park on the roof meaning the July sun and humidity would create a major frizz to my curls. Oh well, the frizz will add to the clown effect that I had apparently been cultivating. I'll be the blubbering, frizzy, town jester.

I was walking toward the elevator when I spotted someone with a gym bag and heard clanking noises. The person was alone, wearing a hoodie with the hood up, in spite of the ninety-degree weather. *Weird.*

I stepped behind a truck to hide my belly and still be able to peek through the windows to see what the person was up to. Maybe I should learn a lesson to not be so nosey, but once I started down the path to investigating, it was difficult to give it up. Kind of like someone telling me to never cook again.

I couldn't tell if it was a man or a woman, but

they were slim and I assumed young—but I wasn't sure why I made that assumption. The person stopped and looked around the roof to see if anyone was watching.

Whatever they were up to, it seemed risky on a hospital parking garage roof to be doing whatever it was they were going to do. They reached in the gym bag and rooted around and I could hear more clanking noises. They pulled a can of spray paint out of their duffel bag and began tagging the cement wall. When the elevator doors opened and they threw their spray can back in the bag and sprinted off.

I called Mick and let him know what I'd just witnessed. He said he'd have a patrol officer stop by and check the hospital security cameras.

I came around the truck I was hiding behind and moved to the elevator when my phone dinged, letting me know I had a new alert from *The Village Herald*, which my friend Bradley ran. I opened the alert to support my friend.

The headline read: *Leavensport Police Receptionist Slain in Cold Blood.*

Wow, that seemed overly sensational. On cue, Gemma, my friend from Tri-City and also Bradley's girlfriend, called me.

"Hey lady, what's up?" I said, knowing the answer.

"I just got the alert. I cannot BELIEVE he stooped so low!" she yelled into the phone. "Also, how are you?" The question came out more sheepishly.

I laughed out loud. "Oh, we're doing fine. Well, as good as can be in this crazy town of ours."

"Yeah, I've heard some of the people here are stirring up some issues over there," Gemma said. "You know, we've had some graffiti here too."

"In Tri-City?" I asked. "No, I wasn't aware."

"Well, Peggy's and my store have been tagged twice now. I think because people know we're friends," she said.

"I am so sorry," I said, not knowing exactly what to say and feeling rage rise at the same time.

"Why?" Gemma said. "You didn't do anything wrong. Peggy and I need to get back to figuring out what is going on with this part of Ohio."

"Same with me and Ava."

"We're not expecting three babies any day, though," Gemma said.

"Yeah, well, more incentive, right?"

"You got it."

"Mick or Ava will be reaching out to you and Peggy at some point with some new information. I don't want to say anything now, though. I'm getting ready to go check on my Aunt Fern." I didn't want to talk on this line knowing we were all getting second flip phones soon.

"Okay, and that new guy in your town—the one who works at the school—" she started.

"Bobby Zane?"

"Yeah, that's him—Peggy said she saw him talking to Mayor Cardinal the other day. I figured I'd mention it to you."

"Thanks for that info." I made a mental note to add it to our I Spy Slides.

"I look forward to hearing from Mick or Ava. We'll get together soon. I'm going to give that man of mine a talking to!" Gemma said. "Talk soon, love."

"Bye," I said, wondering if I should warn Bradley, then deciding not to—he could deal with the fallout on his own.

I finally reached the ICU floor and went to the information desk to see if they could locate my Aunt Fern for me and give me Mayor Nalini's status. The nurse told me there had been no change with his coma yet. Just then, the elevator opened and my Aunt Fern walked in, her face showing zombie-like exhaustion, with my mom and my grandma orbiting her, blabbering at her. She looked utterly helpless. I'd been there many times before myself.

"Mom, Grandma, I've got it from here. You two go get lunch or something," I said, sternly staring hard at them both. They both gave me a we're-your-elder challenging look, but I held my ground and they reluctantly asked both Fernie and me if we'd like anything.

After we declined their offer, I led her to the waiting area, where it was pleasantly quiet, and sat down next to her, holding her hand.

"You don't need to check on me. I'm fine," she said after a few minutes.

"I can leave if you'd rather be alone. I understand that," I offered.

"Nah, I appreciate the few moments of silence, though." She tried a smile.

I nodded and sat.

Several minutes later Aunt Fern said, "You know, he and I discussed marriage. I never thought I'd ever be one for marriage. I've always been happy to be alone and lord knows my family keeps me busy.

"But, Fatin, he was married before and he loved it. He still loves his wife, even though she passed so long ago and I admire and respect that— and her—she sounds amazing."

"Wow, I never knew you two discussed all those things. It's funny how I've aged and I still think of all of you like I did when I was a kid," I said.

"Yeah, well, I never had kids of my own but I'd take a guess you carrying these two is giving you some new perspectives. I imagine you'll grow a lot more and they will make you wiser. I know you've made all of us wiser and I don't say it enough—but I'm thankful for that." She patted my hand.

I swallowed hard and looked away, brushing away a solitary tear.

"I wanted to do Ireland for our honeymoon. I've always wanted to go. You know we have a bit of

Irish in our genealogy, as well as the Cherokee," Aunt Fern shared.

"What a mix!" I said. "Ireland is still a possibility, you know. Don't give up hope."

"Oh, I'm not. I've just needed to get my head back on straight." Aunt Fern had a far-off look on her face, so I sat silently, allowing her time to ponder.

"You know—somehow, as I said, you have inspired me yet again. I need to feel useful at this time and I'm going to give Abbey a call and check on something. Thank you for visiting and for freeing me from those two goofballs we have to endure." She grinned authentically at me this time.

I wondered what she was up to.

Chapter Six

I was finally heading to Cast Iron Creations when I ran into Earl Seevers in the hospital parking lot. I felt my face begin to flame, remembering the compromising position he was in last time I saw him.

"Oh-uh-hey, Mr. Seevers. I was just checking on my Aunt Fern."

"I'm here to check on the mayor's health. Any word?" He didn't seem the least bit embarrassed—which made sense. He and his wife were permitted to do anything they wanted behind closed doors. I was the intruder.

"Still in a coma. Aunt Fern said no one should make any decisions for at least two to three weeks after the surgery as things can change as his brain heals afterward."

"Okay, well—you had something to ask me?"

I stared slack-jawed at him. I knew I did, but I

couldn't remember the question. I could only see him in those black leather shorts with his hands tied by the red satin ribbon to the bed.

"Oh—yeah, right. That's the entire reason I was there to begin with—again, I'm so incredibly sorry," I started.

"It's fine. Your intentions were in the right place, Jolie. Well, if you think of it, give me a call." He began walking away.

"Wait, I remembered!" I said, and he turned back toward me. "What were you and Nancy arguing about at the monthly meeting?"

"Oh, I'm a suspect, am I?" He joked.

"No, Ava and I are just trying to figure things out and you two seemed heated. So, we wanted to know if Nancy is—er—was involved in something," I blurted out, afraid to tell him that it did kind of make him a suspect.

"Aw, I got it." He scratched his head and looked around. "Where on earth did I park?"

Odd. Should I ask the question again? I thought. *Why isn't he answering me?*

"I parked on the roof. The valet wasn't at the station when I came in," I said, waiting.

"Okay, well, I better be going," Earl said.

"You don't want to answer the question?"

"I mean—I can, I guess, but I don't think it has anything to do with what happened to her, so—"

"Haven't the police questioned you about it?"

"You mean Mick doesn't tell you?"

"He can't do that. We have to have boundaries with our jobs," I said, wondering why he was stalling.

"You know, it just feels like gossip is all," he started just as Bobby Zane walked past us and Earl's eyes followed him into the building. "But yes, speak of the devil—you know how Nancy is—she was telling me—well—about Mr. Zane there. I guess he ran a school back in Chicago and had some weird policy and that got him fired from one school. Then he became a board member then from there got into politics or something and Nancy was afraid he was trying to do the same thing here in Leavensport."

"Okay," I started. I wasn't sure I bought all that—it had inconsistencies from what Nancy told me in the kitchen before the Community meeting, but at the same time, I didn't like or trust Bobby Zane and wouldn't be surprised if that was true, especially if he was trying to worm his way into being mayor. "Well, I need to get moving to the restaurant."

"Sure thing, and seriously, Jolie—don't be embarrassed. Bea and I love you and we know you meant no harm." With that, he waved and went on his way.

How could I suspect such a caring, generous man.

I finally made it to the restaurant and was excited to get to spend time in the kitchen cooking for our customers. I waved to Ava and moved to the back to get my apron on, expecting to see Carlos cooking. Instead, Ryder was at the oven, bent over, pulling out a casserole that smelled delicious.

"Oh, hey," I said, noticing he had his hoodie up and tied around his face exactly like the person at the hospital.

"Hello, Jolie—oh, sorry for the hoodie, I'm always cold no matter the temperature. Another reason why a kitchen is where I belong . I can keep warm." He smiled a James Dean shimmer at me.

I mumbled out a speculative noise. "I thought Carlos would be working—and you haven't officially started yet, have you?"

"Oh, I told him he could officially start," Ava said, walking back to the kitchen.

"We should probably discuss all official decisions," I said through gritted teeth.

"What's your problem? Chillax, he's doing great. Carlos had a construction emergency at his new restaurant and Ryder was happy to step in to help out since you were out running errands." Ava cocked her head at me.

"I don't want to create a problem," Ryder said, setting the pan on the stove. "I can take off. I just need to add a little more sauce and give it a stir. Then it's ready for the lunch special today."

"Look at how beautiful that presentation is." Ava jerked her head toward the noodle and chicken creation that did smell wonderful. "Ryder created it—it's Cashew Chicken with Noodles."

"Looks great." I eyed Ava purposely. "We'll get back to you, Ryder."

Ryder nodded and took off out the back door.

"Why are you being so rude to him?" Ava demanded, crossing her arms.

I explained what I witnessed on the roof of the hospital with the figure in the hoodie.

"That's ridiculous. You're just being paranoid." She walked over to the chicken dish and grabbed a fork out of the large basket of disposable tasting utensils and sampled a bite of Ryder's dish. Ava whistled a low note as her brown eyes widened. "Try this and tell me you don't want that man to take Carlos' place when he moves on."

I tasted it and had to admit it was out of this world. He had a flare for making flavors pop in the mouth. "It's great and as long as he isn't some criminal mastermind, then yeah, he's got the job. Right now, I don't know."

"Well, we can't delay the birth of our babies, Jolie. He's our best option—so, unless he's caught and arrested, he's hired." Ava's words were clipped as her jaw jutted forward.

"You can't override me!" I felt panic begin to swirl inside me as the feeling of being overwhelmed began to take over again.

"I can if you're being irrational!"

"I'm not being irrational. I'm being protective of me, you, the townspeople—how is that irrational?"

Ava took a deep breath and let it out slowly. "All I'm saying is, we haven't found anyone else with this level of culinary expertise. I don't think we should lose him because you suspect him of something. Shouldn't everyone be treated as though they are innocent until they are proven guilty?"

Uh, I hated when she was right. I hesitated for a long moment, then flipped my hands up in defeat. "Okay, you win. He's hired. But stop making decisions without consulting me. We make the big decisions together."

"Okay, OKAY!" Ava's head jerked back.

"It looks like he prepped everything for the rest of the day so my work will be light," I said. "I can help out in the front, or let me know if there is any office work you are behind on and I can take care of it between plating."

"Yeah, there are a few bills that'll be due in the next month lying on the desk. You can pay those and get them ready for the mail if you have time."

"Done," I said, plating a few orders I saw, then moving to the little side office off the kitchen. I wrote out the checks, then saw no new orders had come in, so I called Mick.

"Hello," he said.

"Hey sexy," I said.

"Back atcha, gorgeous."

"So—" I started seductively.

"What do you want?" He knew me too well.

"Um, I was wondering if there were any clues at the murder scene at the B&B. Ava and I are looking into some things."

I swear I heard a deep breath—it seemed I made people breathe deeply—which is a good thing, right?

"We found a lot of things and we have to look into it all. Because it was at a public place, there were all kinds of things—trash—a cup from Chocolate Capers, a scrap of a red fabric ribbon, a spray paint can. See what I mean? Lots of things that could be there just as normal debris or litter that was blown around from the storm, and the paint can—we all know there's been spray-painting happening everywhere."

"Right, so it's a question of whether it's a clue or just normal stuff that you'd find any day of the week."

"Exactly, and we can investigate and ask questions, but some people just don't want to talk to the police," Mick started.

"Oh, but someone like Ava or me questioning people may not raise any eyebrows," I said, catching his drift. "We don't make them feel like they could be in trouble."

"This is where you two come in handy," Mick teased.

"Jerk," I joked back.

"Oh, oops," Mick said in an exaggerated fake-worried voice. "I *accidentally* sent a picture of those clues to your phone. I sure hope my wife deletes those *right away*, and doesn't *use them to help her investigation.*"

I grinned and played along. "Don't worry, hubby. I have already deleted those very photos." I made a big show of pretending to tap some buttons. He was a real sweetie for bending the rules for me. I knew it was against his better judgement, but seeing those items would really help me out.

"Good, good—also, seems you may want to visit Betsy soon—it's been a long time since you two have talked."

I scrolled through the pictures and saw the Chocolate Capers cup with an order written on it in barista shorthand. I realized he wanted to know what that order was—but I figured Betsy would readily tell Mick, so I left that task to him. "Eh, I saw her two days ago. Why don't you go get yourself an iced mocha?"

"Um, Jolie—did you get the alert I just got?"

I looked at my phone again and saw that my Aunt Fern had sent an alert to the town group text that there was an emergency meeting at the Community Center in an hour and everyone was strongly encouraged to join. "What's she doing?"

"I wonder if the mayor is okay and she's letting us all know?"

"I'll meet you there."

"First off, I'm sorry for the late notice, everyone."

Aunt Fern started the meeting. I was surprised at how many people showed up. I'm sure there were many businesses in Leavensport with 'Be Back at' signs on their doors like we did.

"Is my uncle okay?" Lahiri, who was usually on the quiet side, spoke up with a crackling voice.

"Oh no, dear, he's still the same. I'm sorry, I didn't think to call you to make you aware that this meeting wasn't about his health." Aunt Fern used a soothing tone.

"Well, then, we all got work to get back to," one of the Zimmerman brothers piped up, elbows wide from his body in frustration.

"Right." She moved on authoritatively. "I wanted to let you all know that I spoke to Abbey about this and right now the doctor isn't sure where everything is headed with Fatin. We need someone to take his place temporarily while he recovers." Aunt Fern bit her lip with a hopeful expression.

"I've held leadership political positions in the past," Bobby Zane piped up immediately.

Wow, that seems fishy... I caught Ava's eye.

"No need," Aunt Fern said. "I've decided to fill in for him and Abbey feels like it's what he would want. Look, there's nothing in the town charter about how to proceed if the mayor is incapacitated, so we all just need to come to an agreement and figure it out together."

I worked to keep my mouth from dropping open, but noticed many others weren't able to quell their disbelief. The aunt I'd always considered to be a bit on the wacky side was showing a level of calmness and professionalism I'd never seen before. Others seemed compelled to listen to her as well.

"Do you even have any experience in politics?" Bobby challenged.

"No, but I've been dating Fatin for quite some time now—" she started.

"And what, he transmitted political experience to you through his lips?" one of the Zimmerman's asked.

"She would do a better job than you would! She would know how to bring people together and not divide us!" Grandma Opal piped up in defense of her daughter.

"I agree," added Bobby. "Seems like someone with experience should step in—and she clearly doesn't fit the bill, Miss Opal."

"I'm sure Jackson Nestle would agree with you," I said, crossing my arms and staring Bobby down.

"We should vote," Abbey spoke up. "All those in favor of Bobby Zane, raise your hand."

I looked around to find very few voting for him—the Zimmerman brothers seemed zealous about voting for him, which ticked me off.

"For Fern Tucker," Abbey called out, then noticed all the hands that raised. "It's settled. Fern, you will take over for Mayor Nalini until we know more on his health."

After the impromptu meeting ended, Ava caught my eye. "Hey, you and I need to meet back up and jot down some notes. I have some more information to share."

"Same here—but there are some things I'd like to look into first." I was thinking about the pictures Mick texted me about possible clues. "I think I'm still in shock that my Aunt Fern is the interim mayor of Leavensport."

Chapter Seven

The next evening was Nancy's funeral service at Converge Life and Faith Church. The strangest thing about it was that she wasn't there to fill us all in on the town gossip. She really was a fixture of our village. The ceremony was respectable enough, and Ava and I behaved ourselves, unlike at other funerals.

Per the norm, there was a reception in the basement afterward. It was just how we did things. The people of Leavensport loved a reason to gather for food.

"So, who will step up as the new town gossip, I wonder?" Lydia said, holding and bouncing Monty in her arms. His chubby cheeks puffed out as a smile spread across his face.

"I vote for Mama Opal." Ava referred to my grandma in her loving way.

"That's a strong possibility," I agreed. "Although Bea could give everyone a run for their money."

"Speaking of those ladies, one of them applied for Nancy's position which is now open," Teddy said, carrying a cup of coffee for himself and likely, Betsy, whom he had arrived with.

"Which one?" Ava asked.

"Bea did but Fern also went for it too," Teddy said.

"Bea? She already works a lot of hours at my restaurant." Mick looked concerned.

Teddy shrugged his shoulders. "Those two aren't the applicants you should be concerned about anyway. There are others."

Mick turned to me with an expression that said, *not you, right?*

"Don't look at me. I already have two jobs and I'm getting ready to birth twins. I have enough on my plate." I took a step back, wide-eyed.

"Your sister, Maria," Teddy said.

I felt a sharp gasp come from Mick as Ava stared incredulously.

"They're in Sicily," Mick said.

"The resume was postmarked from there. I'd say they are on their way back here soon," Teddy said.

"They *have to* know," I said. "Why else would they pick up from their home in Sicily and bring their business here?"

"You don't worry about it. I'll handle it." Mick

squeezed my hand.

I couldn't help but worry. I turned to see who was coming down the steps and saw Ryder with Marissa. Oh well, he was probably getting to know people—why he was finding the worst people to get to know was beyond me. Pregnancy seemed to make me more critical of people.

I heard a weird noise that seemed to be coming from multiple places in the basement and began looking around. I noticed most people looked as mystified as me.

When I glanced at Ava, she was giving me a knowing look, but I didn't know what it meant so I shrugged my shoulders at her.

She held one of the new flip phones that Mick bought everyone up in my face. He put Ava in charge of settings for them and getting them to everyone in our group. Seems like she made the same alert noises for everyone.

I attempted to nonchalantly look at the phone and saw a text for something called the "PURV group" to meet over at Cast Iron Creations and to come from the back alley. That we all needed to make sure we weren't followed.

A few minutes later everyone in our group minus Lia, Darrell, Gemma, and Peggy were in our restaurant's kitchen.

"First off, we should all change our alert noises, so they aren't all the same. Takes away from the spy angle," Bradley said while scrolling through his phone to change the sound.

"The biggest question I have is, why are we called PURV?" Keith's eyebrow raised.

"Oh, so our group name is Pudding Up With Relatives—because we all have to deal with crazy families. But PUWR doesn't make any sense as a quick code word." Ava looked at Keith as if that should have been extremely obvious.

"I mean, PURL could work, or PURT—how about one of those?" I asked, looking at Mick.

"Let's go with PURL," Lydia piped up, agreeing with me for once.

"Hey, Betsy, can I ask you something?" I pulled her aside for a moment, getting out my regular cell. "Do you mind telling me what this order is at your shop?"

I showed her the picture Mick sent to me.

"Oh, that's a triple shot mochaletto, which at my place means three shots of espresso in what is like a caramel macchiato. See the 'P' here, that's a squirt of pumpkin flavoring—only Bobby Zane orders his morning beverage that way."

"Okay, thanks." I made a mental note to add this information to our I Spy Slides as well as telling Mick. So far, Bobby and Ryder were on my suspect list.

"Why?" Betsy asked, but Ava started talking before I could finish the thought.

"So, folks, I called you all here to check that the new phones work. And we're sure that no one can trace these?" She looked toward Mick.

"I bought them over an hour away, with cash, destroyed the receipt, and then removed any GPS tracing from them," Mick said.

"What he means is he's done as much as he can do. There is only so much we are able to do with the Patriot Act—the next best thing is if we drive an hour out of town to buy a new phone after every use and continue to trash phones," Tabitha said.

"This will do." Ava bit her lip.

"I want to get it on record that I don't trust Darrell being in this group," I said. "I wouldn't be surprised if he was the Leavensport mole."

"He isn't old enough to be the mole, but I still don't think we should give him a phone—and we should keep him out of as many meetings as possible," Tabitha said. "We'll make him think he's on the inside without handing him too much information."

"I don't want him in the group either, Jolie," Keith said. "But here we are. Yeah, I chose not to tell him about the meeting today. We will need to invite him to some of them to keep him from getting jumpy, though."

"He'll end up being a mole inside the mole," Ava said.

"Huh?" many of us asked.

"You know, a mole in Leavensport—a mole within our group—a mole within a mole," Ava glanced around, taking in each of our amused faces.

"Makes perfect sense to me," I laughed,

supporting my BFF.

"If it was anyone it would be Darrell," Keith agreed. "Now, be sure to stagger our return to the church so no one suspects anything. It will draw attention if we all come back in a group.

Ava and I hung out at the restaurant, prepping for the morning while the others moved out every so many minutes to head back to the church.

"Have you heard from Chuck since the hospital?" Ava asked while washing mushrooms for the omelet special in the morning.

I was slicing some colored bell peppers when I stopped mid-slice. "I tried to call him because I wanted to talk to him about not being in the twins' lives. But now his number is no longer in service.'" I started slicing again.

"Of course it isn't," Ava snorted. "It's like he knows what you're going to tell him."

My relationship with my biological father was a lifelong disaster-in-progress. This was one of the perks when I couldn't reach him—knowing I got a break from his manipulations. At some point, he'd show back up like nothing ever happened and if I decided to call him on it, he'd apologize profusely while crying and shaking all over—if that was real or a way to manipulate my feelings, well, I didn't know anymore, and I also didn't care.

Mick and Teddy decided to go in and get caught up on some paperwork at the office after the funeral. I went straight home, got into bed, and snuggled up with my journal and pen.

Ava brought Chuck up again tonight.
Everyone kept telling me not to worry, but truth is
I'm more worried about the next time he shows up.
I'd rather it be before the twins arrive because I
want him to know there is no place for him in their
lives. I couldn't help but twitch every time I heard
the phone ring or heard an unexpected knock at
the door. Now, he's made it so I can't reach him by
phone again. The last time that happened, he had a
gambling debt and men trying to find him through
my mom to get him to pay up—was I even ten
then?

I felt emotions beginning to surge, so I changed the topic.

List of Notes to Talk to Ava About

- *Bobby Zane—clue #1—his cup at scene of crime. What Earl said about Bobby in Chicago and his trying to be interim mayor here.*
- *Earl acting so weird when talking to me.*
- *Ryder—I need to make Ava realize there could be something going on with him— the hoodies and leather jacket in July, talking to Marissa.*
- *Zimmermans—they've been way more jerky and hostile toward the Tuckers than usual—should we talk to them?*
- *Clues: pictures—add to slides: cup from Chocolate Capers—order—Bobby Zane; scrap of red material; spray paint can—I think Ryder. The material is what has me confus~~~*

I felt myself nodding off to sleep. Several hours later, I woke up to the sound of Mick's voice in the next room, which was his den. I looked over at the clock which read two a.m. Who could he be talking to? He just had been with Teddy.

I slid off the bed and tiptoed to the adjoining door, trying to hear better. It was slightly ajar and I could see the glow from his computer screen. I couldn't see who—but someone was on the screen.

"Your parents are helping me as much as they can. I have information that can help you and those people you have taken on as family." The voice sounded female and kind of familiar.

"What is it?" Mick asked her.

I could see his muscles tensing from the glare off the screen.

"Now, Micky," said the low, breathy, smoky voice, "you know I'm more than happy to provide information to you, but you've got to do something for me."

"And what's that, Imelda?" Mick sighed heavily.

Imelda? But she was in prison—in Italy. Without thought I started into the room, coming up behind Mick as I heard Imelda speak again.

"I mean, your family can only do so much. I feel like your little FBI buddies could help out a lot more, and trust me when I tell you this information will break everything. And who knows? When I get out, you and I could get some dinner," Imelda said, then her eyes darted up to my face in surprise.

Mick turned abruptly, blinking rapidly as his face went pallid.

"Listen, you Italian Amazon princess, we are MORE than capable of figuring things out without your help!" I whipped my face around to Mick. "Why wouldn't you discuss this with me first? You know my history with her."

Mick's eyes teared up when he heard the hurt in my tone.

"Calm down, Barbie." Then I saw her eyes darken as they rested on my middle. "Oh, wow, I didn't know Barbie dolls could get pregnant."

"You know, it's kind of nice seeing you in a little box like this—kind of like your forever home now, huh?" I spat back at her.

Imelda's face shape-shifted and turned shadowy as the lines of her cheekbones distorted. "I told you once before that you're in over your head. You obviously didn't believe me if you thought getting pregnant by him would be safe for you and that baby."

"I'll make sure you never see the light of day again!" Mick lightly pushed me aside to lean into the screen.

"Micky, come on, we both know how things work here in Italy—I'll be seeing you both sooner rather than later."

With that, she cut off the screen.

"Are you INSANE?" I yelled at Mick. "I mean,

seriously, man—are...you...IN-SANE?" I swore I could see the bright color of blood flash before my eyes as I scrubbed my hands over my face.

"Jolie, breathe, babe—" Mick started.

"Mick, I swear—do NOT tell me how to react to you making a decision to speak to her without consulting me. I know we have boundaries but she has NOTHING to do with that," I said referring to the couple therapies we went through about my PI work and his detective work.

"I know—listen, please," he pleaded.

"Listen, you KNOW she attacked me. You said even though we have boundaries with both our jobs that you'd NEVER use her for information. But okay—I'm done." I crossed my arms and tapped my foot on the floor. "I'm listening now."

"I called my sister to ask her about applying for Nancy's job. I wanted to know what the Milano family angle was there. She told me Mom and Dad are going through zoning legalities to build a jewelry store on part of the new property they purchased behind our restaurant near the Villy Crisis Center—back in the woods—and supposedly my mom has some grand idea to have the town pave a road named after the family."

"What?" My heart began beating harder. Between dealing with Chuck, Mick's parents and knowing there was behind the scenes nefarious activities going on in our town—well—I was beyond a wreck. "Knowing your family, they're planning to build a McMansion back there and who knows what will happen from there."

"Exactly. This is the reason I felt it was *imperative* I contact Imelda. They won't tell me things—I know this from our history. But I know I can get Imelda to tell me things."

"Then you should have discussed that with me FIRST!" I yelled as tears sprang to my eyes.

Mick chewed his bottom lip with sincerity pouring from his eyes. "You're right. I panicked."

I took a breath and slowly and silently counted to ten. "I get anxiety. Mine has been off the charts lately."

"I know that. It's part of the reason why I didn't want to get you involved with Imelda again." Mick took two large steps toward me, bridging our physical gap.

"It's still no justification for not telling me. We have to be open with each other. Trust is most important." I playfully swatted his bare six pack then felt those preggo hormones kick in as I looked up at him.

"No fair," he grumbled, leaning his chiseled, scruffy chin down to my neck and nuzzling it.

"Hmmm?" I murmured, eyes closed.

"You're using your womanly wiles to get your way." He pushed me back toward the bed.

"I never took an oath to play fair in this marriage," I said, shutting the door to the cats.

Chapter Eight

The morning came way too soon for me and the little monkeys were bouncing around in my belly again. Last night started out rocky, but ended in a wonderful way.

"You doing okay this morning?" Mick walked over to kiss me, then the twins.

"I feel like we're on a merry-go-round and I need it to stop for a while so I can take stock and get things in order, but it won't stop." I answered him honestly, the anxiety and weariness coming out in my voice. "I mean—how are we supposed to deal with your family, Chuck, all this criminal activity in town? You and everyone keep telling me to not stress, but—" I held my hands up above my head in an overexaggerated shrug, then realized the hem of my maternity dress rose too high, showing thigh. I put my arms down quickly when I saw Mick peeking.

"First off, stop quoting *Grey's Anatomy* lines—

no matter how wonderful they are," he said. "Second, there is only so much we can do right now. We're in the middle of it all. So, it's one day at a time. You can't communicate with Chuck if you can't find him or reach him. I can't stop my family from moving here and opening a jewelry store—okay. So, we will deal with things as they happen—together."

I took a deep breath. I was one of those people who what-iffed everything and I needed closure. While what my husband said made complete sense to me logically, my emotions had a whole rich inner life of their own—and I tended to be led by them rather than by reason. "I'm trying. Also, how do you know *Grey's Anatomy* lines?"

"I'm only human, Jolie. I rooted for McDreamy and Meredith, too."

I couldn't help but grin. "You never cease to amaze me—also, you and Ava are the only two people who know how to instantly calm me down. I may need you two to give *me* some pointers to use on myself."

"We got your back, sweetie."

"Oh crap! I'm supposed to pick Ava and the girls up—NOW!"

"What girls?"

"Lily, Luna, and Lulu have a vet appointment this morning with Dr. Libby. They need their annual shots and I told her I'd help her wrangle them up and get them in to the vet. We're going to be late!"

"I'm calling the vet to let them know you're running behind. Take your time."

Five minutes later, I called Ava from her driveway. "I'm here—sorry I'm late! Mick called to tell the vet we're running late. You need me to come in or are all three in one carrier?"

Ava was panting loudly in between words as she said, "Wouldn't [*pant*] that be [*pant*] nice? No one is *in* anything...they're all...hiding...under the bed and I...can't reach them with...Little Bo Peep stretching out my...stomach."

"I'm coming in." I hung up the cell and hustled toward her house. I needed to remember to breathe. Trips to the vet with kitties always increased my stress level. *Oh man.* A thought hit me like a ton of bricks. What would I be like when the twins had to go to the doctor and get shots?

I shook the thought off. *Nope, one thing at a time.* I opened the door carefully.

"Hey girls, it's Aunt Jolie—where's my cutie-patooties?" I yelled out in my squeaky cat voice.

I saw two little black faces with green eyes peek around a corner at me as I attempted to bend over to reach out to them, but Ava scooped them up and put them in the carrier and locked it.

"Thanks." She wiped her forehead. "Now, for Luna."

"Okay, well, do NOT open that crate back up. Get another one ready—we don't want to chance anyone escaping until they reach the vet's office where there is professional help."

Ava nodded, heading to get another crate as I padded back toward the bedroom. All the while, two sets of green eyes followed my feet, meowing loudly at me from the crate. It hurt my heart to know they were uncomfortable and afraid. The agony of being an extreme animal lover.

"Luna-Tuna, where's my baby girl?" I asked, creeping into the bedroom. I sat on the bed, praying I wouldn't have to get down on the floor, because we may need to call an ambulance (or a crane) for assistance if it came to that.

I heard a mew from under the bed. "Is that my sweet girl down there?" I peeked behind headboard of the bed, leaning my body over the best I could to reach down to see if she'd come to my hand.

I felt a cold nose hit my fingers as I dangled them and I heard Ava stop at the door, not wanting to make any sudden moves. "What's you doing, sweet girl? Auntie Jolie wants some Luna-Tuna snuggles." I reached to scratch her head while evaluating the width of the space from the backboard to the wall and wondering if I could squeeze her through it if I could get ahold of her. I knew if I failed, we'd have to make another appointment for her and we were both so swamped with so many things right now.

"That's it, baby," I said, rubbing her neck as I felt her move out from under the bed. "Let me pick you up for a hug."

I picked her right up to my chest and cradled

her for a bit before we put her in the crate. Success!

"Oh man, this is one time I'm willing to tell you how awesome you are!" Ava bellowed, hefting the crate with the two as I took Luna.

"Thanks, I think?" I questioned the backwards compliment.

We finally made it to the vet and into the exam room and freed the girls—who now didn't want to get out of the carrier. Typical women.

"Did you give any more thought to the Ryder situation?" Ava asked.

"I mean. Yeah—his food is amazing and if I didn't feel like he could be a suspect then I'd love for him to take over. I just don't know for sure. I don't know—maybe it was a coincidence that someone in a long-sleeved black hoodie with the hood up was spray-painting on the wall of the hospital. I guess we can put a hold on the hire if we don't agree."

"Yeah, the leather jacket and hoodies are strange," Ava agreed. "He only puts the hoodie up sometimes. We had other applicants, but no one cooked like him or had the recommendations he had."

"You have a point with innocent until—"

Dr. Libby came bouncing in in her dog and cat scrubs and her Crocs. "Hello, ladies! Had a bit of trouble with the girls this morning, I heard."

Dr. Libby always sported a long, light brown, ponytail, no makeup, but was still fresh-faced with rosy cheeks, a smattering of light freckles across her nose, and a perky attitude that immediately put nutsos like me and Ava at ease.

"They were so bad. Thankfully, they fell for Jolie's tricks," Ava said.

"I wouldn't call it tricks necessarily," I huffed.

"You used the trust they have for you to get them in the carrier—that's a trick!"

"Whatever it takes," Dr. Libby interjected with a grin, breaking up our verbal sparring. Unfortunately, she was used to us.

"You two still in charge of the yard sale?" Dr. Libby asked.

"We are," I said, "but with the mayor in the hospital, I'm not sure where that stands right now."

"Well, you have an inside track with your aunt as acting mayor," Dr. Libby said.

"True. Hey, if we do it, are you putting anything out for the yard sale if it happens?" I asked.

"I think I'll do a table about pet adoption and I have a bunch returned things that I may put out at a discount, too." She reached for Luna first and turned her around to get her temperature and weight, then checked her ears and heart, and finally gave her the shot.

"Have you ever thought about opening a rescue shelter?" Ava asked.

"You know, we've discussed that here. I'm thinking of getting a partner for the business and hiring an office manager. If and when that happens, then I'd definitely consider it!"

"That would be amazing," I said.

"Did you come up with a kitschy name for the yard sale? You know how Mayor Nalini always insists every festival or community event have a title." Dr. Libby laughed her boisterous, loud laugh.

"Nope, but you just did," I smiled. "Leavensport Annual Kitschy Community Yard Sale."

"A mouthful," Ava nodded. "I love it!"

"Me too, and it's in honor of our mayor, who, as Dr. Libby says—loves a kitschy name!"

A half hour later, we were heading out to the CR-V as Bea Seevers was fast-walking in with a fish bowl in one hand and a bird cage in the other.

"Whoa, you need some help?" I asked, carefully taking the fish bowl she was trying to balance in her hand.

"Oh my, thank you." Bea set the bird cage down on the concrete. "Bringing these guys in for a check-up."

"She examines *fish*?"

"She does for my Bert and she takes great care of Oscar and Donald here, too," Bea said, referring to her two parrots.

"Are they all named after cartoon characters?" I asked.

"Yep, and all the grumpy ones, too. They were always my favorite!" Bea grinned.

"Mine too!" I exclaimed, then changed the subject abruptly. "Did Mr. Seevers tell you about our conversation the other day?"

"You mean about that Bobby Zane. Not one to trust, if you want my opinion," Bea said, reaching down to add a few treats in the bird cage under the dark blanket that covered it to keep them calm.

"I agree," Ava joined in. "But Jolie, the girls are getting antsy—I want to get them home."

"Okay, just a second." I said, then pulled my phone from my tote turned to Bea. "Do you recognize anything in these pictures?"

I scrolled through the pictures Mick sent me of the clues at the B&B.

"No, I don't think so—wait, can you blow this up here?" She pointed to one picture.

I blew it up and her face turned paler.

"What's wrong?" I asked.

"It's just—well—that scrap of red right there. That's the tie to one of my red robes. I know because Earl had my initials sewn in black on it—see?"

"Have you two ever..." I blushed deeply and involuntarily, "...ahem...gotten a room at the B&B?"

Bea gave me a mischievous smile. "No, but that isn't a bad idea." Her face fell back into a worried expression. "What does all of this mean?"

"You go deal with your vet appointment and don't worry. Ava and I will figure it out and we'll let you know what we find." I waved and turned to get

Ava and the girls home so we could head into Cast Iron Creations.

We got back to Ava's and released the babies, watching as they beelined to Delilah, who was fixing their breakfast for them.

"Hey girls, thanks for taking them in today." Delilah smiled at us. "A huge order of acrylics, oils, and watercolors came into the art shop this morning and your new chef, Ryder, was walking by and offered to help me move boxes around. He's a character!"

"Why?" I asked.

"Jolie thinks there's something off about him—" Ava started.

"Oh, because of the hoodies and the jacket in scorching heat?" Delilah giggled and spread her arms, looking at her oversized hoodie she was wearing.

"Yeah, but you don't have your hood up inside. And you have every right to wear a sweatshirt because the air is blasting in here. Right, so he's a bit strange," I said.

"Yeah, but he's actually a great artist. He told me about some of his artwork he used to do in California. He had some pictures of things that hit galleries for sale. It's not bad. I told him to come see me if he gets back to it." Delilah tapped through her phone to show us some of the pictures of art he had forwarded to her.

"Those are huge!" Ava said.

"Extremely large canvases and he does his drafts on huge poster boards is what he told me," Delilah said, scrolling through the pictures.

"Wait, what's that?" I asked.

"Oh, he left his gym bag of paints by the painting, I imagine." Delilah kept scrolling.

"Were they cans of spray paint, by chance?" I asked.

Ava narrowed her eyes at me.

"Sure, if you are using a large canvas like he is, then that's a common paint to use." She looked back and forth between Ava and me. "Listen, he's new around here. I'm sure he's not behind the graffiti here in town."

"See?" Ava leaned over to kiss her honey.

"Okay, I'm just saying, is it really all a coincidence?" I saw the death glare Ava was giving me so I dropped it for the moment. "We do need to go question Bobby Zane and maybe Mr. Seevers again after what Bea told us this morning."

"Also, Caleb, Asher, and Nestle—and we can *talk* to Ryder in a *careful* way to see if we can find anything out," Ava responded slowly, which made me aware she still wasn't buying my thoughts about him.

"Why Caleb, Asher, and Nestle—did you find something out about them that you didn't tell me?"

"No, but why not? They always seem to be involved in some way." Ava shrugged.

"I mean, yeah, behind the scenes. No one can

ever prove anything, though." I sighed.

"Have to keep trying," Delilah said while gathering kitty dishes to clean.

I looked down at my phone. "Oh boy."

Ava looked down at hers as well. "Aunt Fern is taking her duties as mayor seriously. Another meeting tonight at seven. Should we close early again?"

"We can play it by ear and see how busy we are," I said.

"I apologize for calling everyone here again so soon after our last meeting," my Aunt Fern started, looking professional in her navy pin-striped suit dress and pantyhose, set off with a chunky, red-heeled shoes.

"Very smart-looking outfit," Ava whispered.

I nodded. In the end, we had decided to close early because just about everyone in town stopped in this afternoon to ask if we knew what the meeting was about. We didn't, but many stayed for a meal or got one to go. I may need to have Aunt Fern do this more often as a marketing ploy.

"I need everyone to listen carefully. Mayor Nalini has started to come to from time to time," she announced as the crowd of townspeople became animated with chatter.

"Again, please listen." She banged the gavel that Mayor Nalini always liked to use in meetings and everyone giggled a little and then settled down.

"I've spoken to Lahiri," she held a hand out toward her, "and she and other family members have given me permission to share that the doctor feels he could make a full recovery. It will take some time and he's not completely out of the woods yet. When he comes to, they are helping him communicate for now with a tablet of letters. They asked if he saw the shooter. Good and bad news. The bad is the gunman was masked. The good, Fatin is able to use the tablet and remembered the shooting, meaning his mind wasn't altered or affected." Aunt Fern gulped in the middle of the last word then turned away to wipe the tears streaming from her eyes.

"Wow, it sounds like he really does have a ways to go," Ava commented out loud.

"He does, but he will survive. Also, Fitan told me to tell you all we need to carry on and be a community. I've decided the community yard sale is still happening." Aunt Fern paused and choked up. She turned her head slightly to the side and coughed to cover her emotions.

After a moment, she pushed her shoulders back and shook her head and said in a strong tone, "I want you all to be assured that I've looked into the legalities here. I had Fatin's attorney meet me at the hospital to witness the conversation I had with our village's mayor."

"Who is his attorney? I'd like to hear that from him," Bobby Zane spoke up.

"Well, Mr. Zane, the Mercurio law offices

handle the mayor's legal issues. They are a husband-and-wife team and *her* name is Becca Mercurio." She took a breath, then scanned the crowd. "Jolie? Where is that niece of mine?"

"I'm here," I said quietly, barely holding a hand up as people turned to stare—which I hated.

Meanwhile, Ava boisterously yelled, "She's right here," and proceeded to point obnoxiously down at the top of my head, just in case anyone needed a visual as to my whereabouts.

"Looks like you need to get busy on putting this thing together. We'd like to have it this weekend," Aunt Fern said casually. Then she gracefully moved on to other business about the graffiti and a sign war that supposedly started in Tri-City that some people in our town were participating in.

"Um, hello, just a minute—THIS weekend?" I interrupted, not worried about all eyes on me for once. "I can't do that!"

At that moment, my second phone blew up. I paused to look through the messages. It was everyone in our PURL group, saying they'd help me get it going. I took a deep breath of relief and smiled, reassured.

"Sorry, Aunt Fern, never mind, I'm good." I turned to Ava. "What did she say about a sign war?"

Chapter Nine

After the meeting let out, Ava and I were walking by a group where one of the Zimmerman brothers was talking about the sign war. I had not heard anything my Aunt Fern said after realizing I had a little more than a week to plan, set up, and execute this community yard sale.

"They don't got nothin' on you, Zed," Timmy Meadows hollered from the back of the group of men.

"Excuse me, what's this—Zed—you started the sign war with Tri-City?" I asked, noticing Ava cross her arms with a speculative look on her face.

Although Ava and I verbally sparred ninety-nine percent of the time, it was all in fun and both of us were opposed to true controversy—we always preferred to try to find common ground if possible. Plus, we had friends in Tri-City—we didn't want to be associated with a town that was trying to bully the citizens of the nearby city.

"I didn't start anything," Zed replied. "They started it with that stupid billboard on the highway by the mall they just put up. So, I put my own sign up!"

"What sign?" Ava asked.

"They wrote something like—what was it, Zander?" Zed asked his brother, who wore the same blue tank top as his brother, making it more difficult to tell the two apart with their matching ZZ Top beards and thick, feathered locks of salt-and-pepper hair cascading down their backs.

"It said, 'The Tri-City Tiger's motto is simple—you be nice to us or we'll tear out your throat.'" Zander said.

"That seems aggressive—what did your sign say?" Ava said.

"You get it. Oh, it said, 'Don't Mistake My Kindness for Weakness. The Beast in Me is Sleeping NOT Dead!'" Zed said to Ava, flexing his chest muscles smugly.

"Actually, I don't *get it*. I mean, yeah, what 'they' did wasn't nice, but you're escalating the situation," Ava said, using air quotes for "they."

"She's right. No one knows for sure who created the sign. One thing we do know for sure is that not every single person who lives in city limits got together and created, and paid for the sign." I flung my hands up and then dropped them, slapping my legs for emphasis.

"Well, *not every single person* in Leavensport

deserves that kind of bullying," Zander shot back, stomping over to tower over me.

"So, you two big, burly dudes felt bullied by a—billboard?" My tone may have taken on a wee bit of sarcasm—I could tell from the red flush creeping up their necks that the brothers as they picked up on it.

"No one gets away with harassing this town," Timmy Meadows bellowed in true mob mentality.

"Guys, first off, be quiet and use your brains—" Ava leaned into the group of men. Even though she wasn't taller than any guy in that group, she somehow managed to look threatening and many of them backed up.

"You are readily admitting to being intimidated by a sign. Think about how utterly silly and ridiculous that is, then think about what Jolie said. You don't know who wrote or paid for it—"

"Yeah! Who did pay for it?" I interrupted. "That might be who's behind the graffiti!"

"Thank goodness I mentioned it," Ava said, giving the men the side-eye. Leave it to Ava to take the credit. "Why are you trying to keep this stupid Tri-City-versus-Leavensport war alive—ever since Ralph was poisoned here, things keep getting worse. Can't we just let it go?"

"It will fizzle out if you don't add fire to it," Ryder said, walking up to the conversation. "Actually, your aunt gave me an idea to help you with the community yard sale that may help defuse the-city-versus-the-town sign war."

Ava nudged me from behind—definitely a see-I-told-you-he's-a-good-guy nudge. Yes, I can tell what she's thinking by a nudge.

"They ain't gonna stop. I'm telling ya'll right now—they ain't gonna stop!" Zed bellowed, hitting a fist on the table, causing those around him to jump.

"What's that?" I gave Zed the stink eye, then ignored his toddler mantrum, directing my question to Ryder.

Ryder followed my lead, ignoring Zed, and said, "Well, we could start a 'sign truce' for the yard sale. You know, just for fun—you start it with a business nearby and others can jump in if they want—but keep it light and funny, then we can make some flyers about the 'sign truce,' inviting people from the city to the yard sale or to join, if you think there's time?"

"I mean, there's definitely *not* time, but I may pass it on to Gemma and Peggy and see if they want to join—" I started.

"Right, they can ask around if others want to bring anything—it extends the offer and builds a bridge." Delilah had walked up with Mirabelle and Spy trailing behind.

I saw Zed and Zander begin to squawk again but even those boys loved Mirabelle and would not risk upsetting her by carrying on in her presence.

Ava and I moved to hug our hostess-with-the-mostess, Mirabelle, who was a twenty-something-year-old woman with a developmental disability.

She was never far from her seeing-eye dog, Spy. Ava's eyes darted to the Zimmermans, daring them to say anything. They took that as their cue to leave.

"Our very own Miss Mirabelle had a brilliant idea." Delilah smiled toward Mirabelle.

"That doesn't surprise me one bit," I said as Ava nodded and we faced her, ready to hear the plan.

"Yep, war is dumb—" she began.

"Agree," I said, giving her a high five.

"So, when I get sad or mad, Delilah has me draw to help me. The graffiti is like art, but it's mean things. Delilah also taught me we can fix any mistakes we make. Those mean pictures can be fixed to be pretty art." Mirabelle shrugged like it was the simplest thing in the world.

Ava and I looked at each other and we both had tears welling up in our eyes. It *was* a simple thing. Unfortunately, people manage to screw it up somehow—me included. One time, someone called Mirabelle a name in front of Ava and me. We almost ripped their faces off we were so angry. But Mirabelle calmly told them they were wrong—she wasn't that word. She gave them other words to use and told them she hoped they would make a nicer decision in the future. This came from Mary, her mom, who was a supermom I knew I'd never be. I hated the thought that people thought Mirabelle and others like her had something wrong with them. Seems to me, they are the answer to most of the world's problems—that thought process is priceless.

"I LOVE that idea." I hugged Mirabelle again, leaning to kiss her on her head. "You're amazing. I love it."

"Where did those smelly boys run off to?" Ava wondered. "Mirabelle, come with me so you can tell them your idea—we'll start with their signs they want to put up!" She grabbed Mirabelle's arm as Spy followed them.

I had to admit I was still skeptical about Ryder, but his idea about the sign truce was a good one. Also, he and Carlos committed to working as many shifts as they could handle the rest of this week so Ava and I could focus on the community yard sale.

Betsy was kind enough to create a list of things with me that needed to be done before this coming weekend and she assigned tasks to our PURL group. I kept forgetting what the *r* and the *l* stood for, then I'd text or ask Ava and she'd remind me: Pudding Up With Relatives. Sometimes I liked that she always wanted to create fun names for everything—other times, not so much.

My first assignment was getting our sign up to get the sign truce underway. Obviously, I wanted to direct the sign to Sir Scratch A Lot vet. Dr. Libby had already offered to keep the truce going, as had many other businesses in town. That was thanks to Mirabelle and Delilah, who were taking over defusing the Tri-City and Leavensport war that had been going on for close to a year now.

I went out to the pylon sign where we kept weekly specials updated and took those down for this week. I got this sign truce started with, "Hey, Sir Scratch A Lot, do you need us to create a cast iron dish for your Hissing Booth at the community yard sale this Saturday and Sunday?"

Once I got the sign finished, I texted Dr. Libby to let her know. I saw her pop her head out of the side door to look and grinned at me and gave me a thumbs up. I had parked in the alley behind the restaurant and walked around the sidewalk to the alley. Suddenly, I saw new graffiti on our restaurant wall. This time it was a pretty decent picture of Tony the Tiger with the words, Tri-City Tigers are like Frosted Flakes. We're GREAT!

I felt my nostrils begin to flare, then I took a deep breath in and thought about Mirabelle. Okay, first off, whoever did the Tony the Tiger did great work—*no pun intended*, I thought to myself, then giggled uncontrollably at how funny I was. As I bent over, laughing at myself, I noticed something shiny laying near a dumpster and snapped out of my stupor and walked over to it. It was another empty paint can. I went to my car and found a napkin in the console to pick up the can, plus a bag in the back seat to stuff it in for safekeeping.

I looked back up at the sign—it was positive and didn't say anything about Leavensport in any negative way.

I sent Ava the picture. *I think we can leave this one.*

Yeah, I agree. We could use this for Mirabelle's idea. Delilah could add a cartoon lion that says, "I agree!" next to it.

My phone rang and I thought it would be Ava, but it was Mick calling.

"Hey, sexy," I started.

"Jolie, it's actually Teddy using Mick's phone." He coughed uncomfortably.

I felt my face turn multiple shades of red. "Oh-uh-I thought—well—" I sputtered.

"Sorry, but I heard you all are going to mess with the billboards."

"Only the ones that are negative—just to make them positive."

"You can't do that—you can't deface property others paid for."

I gulped—DUH! We were all on board because it was Mirabelle, I never gave a thought to the legalities. AVA!

"Hey, I gotta go!" I hung up and called Ava as quickly as I could.

"Hey, were you tired of texting?" Ava said, picking up after the first ring.

"No, listen, you didn't mess with any signs yet, right?"

"Not yet, but I've got my eye on one!"

"Don't!" I pleaded, then explained what Teddy just told me.

"That is—" Ava started to protest then thought

better of it and took a long pause. "Yeah—that is illegal. Wow."

"Quick! Make sure Delilah and Mirabelle aren't doing that!" My voice rose two octaves.

"I texted Delilah as soon as you said that. She already texted this back—I forwarded it to you," Ava said.

"Hold on—" I looked down at my phone.

Yeah, that's illegal. Please tell me you and Jolie are NOT in jail right now.

"For the next few months, we still have a good excuse for our idiocy," I said flatly.

"What will we do after that?" Ava asked.

We both laughed out loud.

"Oh yeah, I wanted to tell you that Delilah's parents paid for a billboard by the mall near the sign that got the Zimmermans all upset. Delilah, Mirabelle, and some other art students are heading there now to create a big mural. I may text her the picture from our building you texted me and have her add the lion with the 'I agree' there. What do you think?"

"I think Mirabelle will be proud of that! Great idea!"

"Are you being punny with the whole Tony the Tiger thing?" Ava's voice had a knowing tone.

I hated she was so quick to catch it. "Maybe."

She knew me so well.

🌶

I decided to eat lunch in our restaurant when Mick texted that he had gotten caught at work and couldn't meet me at home.

It worked out well because Bobby Zane and Caleb stopped in for lunch and I took it upon myself to join the two at their table.

"Um, we're waiting on a third," Caleb said.

"Nestle or Asher?" I asked.

"Asher," Caleb tipped the chair back on the rear legs and crossed his arms.

"No problem. I own the place—we have lots of chairs to spare. So, Bobby," I turned my head to him, "I'm curious what made you want to jump on the opportunity to stand in for Mayor Nalini's spot. I mean, you haven't been in this town that long."

"Oh—well—I—uh—" Bobby stammered, side-eyeing Caleb.

"Wait, did Jackson Nestle or one his henchmen here push you to do this?" I blatantly asked.

"What? N-n-no." He continued to stumble over his words. "I was involved in politics back in Chicago so I thought I could help out for a month or so. That's all." Bobby looked down at his hands.

"Time's up." Asher stood over me.

"Excuse me? You're standing in my restaurant. What exactly do you mean by that?" I stood up, staring at him, causing him to take two steps back from my protruding belly of babies.

"I mean, time's up—to them—we can dine somewhere else." Asher tipped his head, letting

Bobby and Caleb know they were to follow him, which both did immediately.

I noticed they didn't pay for their drinks. I pulled some money out of my purse and laid it on the table to cover the beverages and a tip for Magda.

I looked over my list. I had gotten several things going today. I wanted to visit the mayor before heading home.

I thought about walking to the hospital as it wasn't that long of a walk, but the ninety-degree weather while being pregnant was too much for me to take. I got into the CR-V and blasted the air conditioner. As always, I tried the trusty valet and this time the pimply faced string-bean of a kid was there again.

It was odd I'd never seen him around town, but with new buildings going up and the progress on the mall, there were more and more unfamiliar faces in town every day. I guess that was one reason the Zimmermans were angry about people in Tri-City. Many people in town felt the urban sprawl was something being pushed on us by Tri-City politicians to put more money in their pockets.

By the time I finished that train of thought, I'd reached the ICU. I smiled and asked the nurse at the nurses' station about Mayor Nalini.

"He was put in a regular room this morning," he said cheerfully.

"Wow, that's great news!"

"Yep, he's still in and out of consciousness from the meds they have him on for the pain. Keep that in mind," the nurse added.

He gave me his room number and I hopped back on the elevator to go up one floor. When the elevator doors opened, I saw Lahiri standing in the hallway, talking to Magda—who I was shocked to see, since she was just at the restaurant. I looked at my watch and realized her shift had ended. Magda looked to be consoling Lahiri about something and the two were giving each other soulful looks.

"Hey ladies, is everything okay?" I asked. "Did Mayor Nalini take a turn for the worse?"

"No, he's doing well. He's a little dopey from pain meds though," Lahiri said. "I was telling Magda that Jackson called things off with me."

Seemed like a good thing to me, but I said, "I'm sorry. I know that's rough."

"His loss," Magda said.

Did I notice a look of interest on Magda's face?

"Well, I want to go in and check on him. I'll see you two later," I said, walking toward the mayor's room. He was laying in the bed, looking very sleepy but aware of his surroundings.

"Hi, Mayor Nalini," I said softly. "It's Jolie Tucker. You'll be happy to know that Aunt Fern is doing a fabulous job filling in for you. She has the entire town working on this community yard sale this weekend." I put my hand on his arm.

The mayor mumbled incoherently. I couldn't

make out what he was saying.

"It's okay, you don't need to try and talk. I just wanted to see you. I—the entire town has been so worried about you. Especially Aunt Fern—"

The mayor's mumbles became panicky. "Fernie! Fern danger..."

"How is she in danger?" I tried to gently rouse him but he seemed to doze off. My bladder was ready to burst and I momentarily thought about running out to the hall to use the public restroom, but the mayor's restroom was right there.

Oh, screw it! I thought as I ran to the tiny bathroom within the hospital room and shut the door. I didn't think Mayor Nalini could get out of bed and come in here right now—I should be good.

I heard someone moving around in the room and assumed it was the nurse. *Whew, what a relief!* I thought as I stood up from the commode. I quickly washed my hands. I wanted to make it back out before the person left. If it was a nurse, I wanted to ask how long the mayor normally slept and if there was a better time of day to come when I could speak to him. I needed to know what he meant about my Aunt Fern and danger.

I pushed the bathroom door open and saw a hooded figure holding a syringe standing over the mayor, getting ready to inject the contents into the mayor's IV.

"What are you doing?" I yelled, rushing toward the hooded invader.

The person turned quickly and threw the syringe at me, causing me to duck. Then they pushed me to the floor and ran out of the room.

Chapter Ten

I was struggling to get up, my rotund stomach making me feel like a turtle on its back, so I reached for the call button that was hanging off the side of the bed. A nurse came rushing in and helped me to my feet. The first thing I did was text Lydia to see if she was in the hospital and if so, to come to the mayor's room.

"Jolie, are you okay? I texted Mick and Ava that you were hurt," Lydia said, kneeling next to me. "Let me help you to a room where you can be examined fully by a doctor."

"No need for that, I'm fine." I waved to the nurse leaving. "Listen, in case anyone else comes in—I need you to take this and see what it is. Whoever was here was trying to put this in the mayor's IV." I handed the tissue-wrapped syringe to her.

"Okay, I need to call Teddy and have someone stationed to watch the mayor," declared Lydia. "I'll be nearby until Mick or Ava get here, then I'll go have this checked out at our lab. I'm going to get you a glass of water and make a couple of calls. I'm going to be right outside the door, then I'll get you to a room."

I sat back and took a breath, rubbing my stomach. My heart was racing. I realized now why everyone was so concerned with Ava and I being wrapped up in all this while we were pregnant.

Mick launched through the doorframe. "What's going on? Have you been checked yet?" In his hurry to rush to my side, he almost slid into me, falling to the ground beside me.

"I'm okay," I said, hugging him. I needed to be consoled. I hated to admit that I felt vulnerable. I'd spent so much of my life being a pleaser. The last few years, I'd finally grown a backbone and started to fend for myself. It had been a while since I'd felt helplessness.

"Okay, we have a hospital security guard outside this door until Teddy can make permanent arrangements. Now, let's get you checked out in a room, Jolie, and I'll take care of this." Lydia dangled the tissue with the syringe in it as Mick helped me up to follow Lydia to a room.

"Yo, I'm right behind, following," I heard my BFF yelling from down the hall.

"We're okay, Ava," I yelled over my shoulder, allowing Mick to take on some of my weight as I leaned into him. I was feeling the fall on my knees and I may have twisted an ankle.

"The doctor will be in soon. You both have my cell number—call if anything happens." Lydia walked out, shutting the door behind her.

Ava pulled out her lightweight Surface laptop and sat down, pulling up the I Spy Slides. "You know we'll be waiting forever on a doctor. We can finally take a minute to get caught up on the case."

"Good idea," I replied.

"Whoa, let's just let her rest," Mick said, putting a hand up to Ava.

"No, I'm fine. My knees and my one ankle are sore. I'm in a hospital. It's fine. Now, listen—" I moved to a lounging position as Mick took a couple of pillows and propped them behind my back and my head. I settled in and continued to explain what had just happened, finishing with telling them that Lydia is testing whatever fluid was in the syringe right now.

"Mmmm—" Mick made a higher pitched noise. "Technically, you should have waited until the police arrived so we could admit that as evidence and then get it tested in our lab—"

"Are you kidding me right now?" Ava's head topped down to her chin as she eyeballed my hubby.

"I'll tell Teddy I ordered it as I knew she could get results better than if we sent it in through proper channels. I'll get a slap on the wrist."

"Sorry," I said.

"Okay, I noted all that. I also finally uploaded

the pix of clues you texted me. AND I even added your thoughts about Ryder, even though I still don't buy it," Ava said.

"What about Mrs. Seevers saying that the red ribbon had her initials on it and Mr. Seevers' behavior with me and what he told me about Bobby?" I asked.

"Whoa, you never told me about that, Jolie." Mick stood rigid. "Which picture?" He pulled his cell out, scrolling through the hundreds of cat pictures to get back to the clues.

I pointed to the picture he wanted to see, thinking back to him "accidentally" sending them to me so Ava and I could question some people and be in the know.

"But even if zoom in, you still can't make it out completely." Mick squinted.

"I know, but she recognized it. I'm sorry—so much has been going on," I said.

The doctor came in at that moment and checked me over and sent me over to another room for X-rays on my ankle and knees to be safe. They had to get out the huge, full-body lead apron to cover my swollen bump. I returned back to the room about forty minutes later to find my aunt, grandma, and mom all gathered with Mick, Ava, and now Delilah as well.

"Everything's okay—ask him," I gestured at the doctor as I pushed myself out of the wheelchair that they demanded I sit in.

"She's good and the babies are too," the doctor said. "We did a full checkup. She'll have some bruising from the fall, and she should take it easy."

"This is all my fault," Aunt Fern said. "I shouldn't have pushed you on this yard sale thing."

"That has nothing to do with what happened. Good heavens," I said. "Besides, my understanding is that everything will be set up and ready to go by this evening. We really need to do something for Betsy. She took it upon herself to take charge and assign responsibilities to everyone."

"Knock, knock—oh, this is too many people," Lydia said, walking in and holding up a paper, letting me know she had information.

"Right, can Lydia and I have a bit of time?" I looked at my family, who all began moseying past me, giving me hugs and kisses on their meandering way out of the door. Ava and Mick stayed behind.

"So, the syringe contained 200 milligrams of Pavulon, which causes paralysis and would create respiratory arrest—also, keep in mind only 100 milligrams is used for lethal injections in our state," Lydia said, reading from the paper.

"Are you sure that's what it is?" Mick asked, reaching for the paper. "I'm going to tell Teddy I asked you to do this. Can I keep this?"

Lydia nodded. "That's what the lab tech found. Why?"

"That's one of the drugs used for the lethal injection," Mick informed us. "There are three things administered. Pavulon, and potassium chloride to stop the heart, and midazolam for sedation—but not in that order, of course."

Ava was typing away, occasionally pausing to ask Mick to spell out some of the technical terms.

"So, whoever did this—did they only want to create paralysis or were they planning to kill the mayor?" I wondered out loud.

"We've not been able to tell if they were trying to kill Nancy and the mayor got in the way or the other way around," Mick said.

"Looks like they wanted the mayor," Ava said.

"Or both of them," I piped up.

"Hey, who's the warden over at Tri-City Correctional Institution?" Ava asked while typing something.

"What are you thinking?" I asked, wishing I could see what she was writing.

Ava held a finger up to me, then continued clacking away.

"Um, something Shuttleworth," Lydia said. "I know because of everything that happened with my dad recently." She was referring to the long story of her dad, who was recently released from prison after it was discovered he had been framed for something he didn't do and imprisoned for years.

"Olin," Mick said. I suspected that he didn't know that because he was in the police force. I bet he knew it because of his brother, who was also Monty's father, Marty Milano.

"Right—why didn't we think of that sooner?" I slapped my own forehead. "A lot of key players converge in that prison! Noah ended up getting killed in there. Marty's in there, and, Lydia—your dad was. How long has this guy been in charge there?"

"I don't know, but that's something we need to find out," Ava noted just as the door opened and Delilah slid into the room. "Also, who paid for that sign by the mall."

"Speaking of..." Delilah scooted over to me, showing me a picture on her phone of the sign her and her art students put up of the mock Tony the Tiger graffiti that was on our restaurant.

"Wow, you all do great work. I love this added line!"

The art students added a note to Tri-City: "Leavensport villagers love all people equally."

"Well, most of us do," I said, thinking of the Zimmermans.

"Okay—so we're all here. Why don't we do this thing already?" Ava asked.

"What thing?" I asked.

"Lydia can bring the thingy in and see what the sex of the babies are," Ava blurted out.

"Really? I want to know!" Delilah squealed with glee.

Mick looked at me, shrugging his shoulders. "What do you think? We've been debating for a while now."

"Well, it *would* give us time to choose colors and decorate and buy stuff in advance," I said. Everyone knew I loved to organize. "Let's do it," I grinned. "We'll have some good news to share at the yard sale this weekend."

Lydia rolled in the machine as the technician followed, getting ready to give Ava and Delilah the news first.

As the technician moved the wand around on Ava's belly, we all leaned forward, trying to interpret the shapes and shadows on the screen.

"It's a girl!" Lydia called out.

I sat up and clapped. "Yay for girls!"

"Okay, you're next." Lydia rolled the machine over to the bed I was lying on.

I was a bit nervous to find out for some reason. I took a shaky breath in, but felt better seeing Delilah and Ava's smiles.

She put the gooey gel on my stomach, which was cool at first touch, then warmed quickly with the friction of the handpiece.

"Whoa, there's one... and... two ladies in the house over here! Lots of girls." Lydia grinned.

"Oh wow, I'm completely outnumbered!" Mick said, laughing and hugging me.

I started crying from the reality of it all and Lydia and the technician ducked out to give us our time.

"I'm sorry," I sniffed, speaking to those left in the room. "I'm happy. I just—I don't know—it's weird. I'm so happy. I've known I was pregnant...but hearing the sex of the girls—uh, the 'girls!' Thinking about if that person would have hurt me or them or injected me with that stuff—it makes me—" I took a breath able to keep myself from getting sick this time. After a second, I recovered and continued. "Whew! Okay. I'm okay. Maybe this whole sickness thing is getting better. Well, I want to get home and get in bed. I need to rest up for this yard sale."

We had a huge banner made and hung between trees in the Leavensport Circle near the pool that had a nice hiking path that led to the park on the east side of town. It read *Leavensport Annual Kitschy Community Yard Sale,* which made for a huge sign.

Nina and her son, Luis, had a booth next to ours with some bakery items for sale, plus she was selling some old baking equipment that still looked like it was in good shape. I saw Ava hanging around their booth, acting oddly.

"Does she have any cast iron?" I asked as Ava walked back to our booth with thumbs flying as she typed on her phone.

"I dunno," she mumbled.

"You were just over there looking!" I exclaimed.

"Oh, that. I took a pic of them and texted it to my sister, Lolly. I want to see if anyone recognizes him or Nina," she said, referring to the fact that their last name Sanchez, which was one of the biggest and oldest families in the Dominican Republic, where Ava's family was from and where they currently resided. They had lived in Leavensport most of her life and had relocated for her dad's job a few years back.

I heard a bit of a ruckus and looked up to see Baggie and Myrtle, our dueling town troubadours, trying to set up in the center of the circle to perform.

Baggie's cocker spaniel, Boo, was next to him, howling at Myrtle, who was shushing the dog. I found out recently that Myrtle had ten cats. I didn't think there was anyone in the running for my title as crazy town cat lady, but she may have me beat.

I looked over at the Leisure Library and noticed they joined in the sign truce and had a picture of our Sammy Jr and Bobbi Jo as well as a pix of Ava's three black cats with a sign that read, "Hey, J&A—they're in your local library. CHECK THEM OUT!"

I laughed at the pun 'check them out.' I was happy to see so many businesses taking part in the fun. The library had lots of books on cats sitting out for sale, as well as some on dogs, and many other great titles.

I saw Devonte making his way to our booth. "Hey ladies, I'd like to purchase some of that fruit cobbler and an icy lemonade, please," he said, looking around and smiling at the colorful displays. "Wow, this little village has such a sense of community. Nothing like I ever had in my neighborhood."

"Hey, you," I leaned over the table, whispering, while adding ice to the glass, "have you heard from Lia lately?" Devonte worked for Lia at the Villy Crisis Center. Everyone believed he ran it, but really Lia was the one who ran it behind the scenes, using him as the face of the organization.

"Actually, she's taking advantage of this yard sale this weekend and doing something in the tunnels under the mall," Devonte said. "Supposedly, there have been rumors that more than construction is going on down there."

"We pretty much knew that to be true. Are we sure it's safe?" I poured the lemonade, then waited until he took a huge swig, then refilled it.

I made myself and Ava a glassful too, so we stayed hydrated. Mick and Delilah had put an awning over our booth to keep it shaded and bought us battery-powered fans to help us stay cool.

"I actually came here to tell you I found something in one of those boxes that Nestle donates to the center," Devonte said.

"What is it?" I asked as Ava handed him a huge helping of our tart strawberry blueberry and peach cobbler.

Devonte laid something on the table with cash over it. "It's under the money." He waved and walked off.

I looked at Ava then picked it up. "It's gambling

chips," I said, confused.

"There isn't a casino in Tri-City," Ava said.

"Maybe not yet?" I asked, flipping the chips around in my hand, then pocketing them. "Hold on, can you watch things for a few minutes?"

"Sure," Ava said.

I went searching for Devonte with a thought. I found him near Baggie and Myrtle, who had eventually opted to perform together. Baggie was doing a jazz rendition of "Little Girl Blue" as Myrtle performed gorgeous vocals for the Nina Simone song. It was beautiful.

"Hey, I wanted to ask you something." I pulled at Devonte's elbow. "Those chips—wouldn't someone just find them when sorting through the boxes? Do you sort through them?"

"Oh no, some of the boxes he brings are marked to go to the Tri-City Correctional Institution. A lot of the people we house and help out come from that prison, so we like to give back. The only reason I found them is one of the boxes ripped while I was putting it in the van to the jail and some of those chips fell out."

"Are they worth anything?" I asked.

"Haven't you been to a casino? That's what you use to redeem for cash."

My blue eyes widened as my head tilted back, making my blonde curls bounce on my bare shoulder. I shrugged and adjusted my tank top up, which was riding up.

"You would probably have to look up the serial number, but they look old and beat up, so I'm guessing they're expired. Once a casino retires chips, they can't be turned back in for money. Some people collect them, though, or keep them to play at home. But they aren't worth more than a few dollars for a whole set." Devonte grabbed one of the chips and turned it over in his hand, thinking for a few moments.

"They might let the prisoners play games with them?" he pondered, looking at the chip, then turning his dark eyes to me.

"Got it, yeah, but I doubt the prisoners would be encouraged to bet in any way—I mean, that could cause some fights. Right? Or am I overthinking it?" I said, feeling the chips in my pocket. More connections, still not a lot of answers.

"I don't know. I get what you're saying, but I'm sure there are a lot of things that go on in prison that the guards or the warden don't know about— and I'm positive some turn a blind eye, especially if they are being paid to do so," Devonte said.

"Good point." I nodded my head as Devonte waved and jogged off. I watched as he slowed down and greeted someone. The person looked male but I didn't recognize him and he had his hood up so I couldn't be sure. The two grabbed hands and strolled toward the pool area.

Aww, does Devonte have someone special?

I was walking back to our booth, excited and happy about the great turnout for the yard sale. The weather was cooperating, although humid and hot. I saw a lot of teens over at the pool and wished I could get up the courage to put a bathing suit on to take a dip.

"Where'd you go?" Ava asked, fanning herself and chugging some lemonade.

"Oh I—ahhh!" I stopped talking and squealed as I got squirted in the back with a steady stream of water from a shirtless boy wearing a tiger mask. I held my hands up as if I was surrendering and saw Ava doing the same.

The boy ran and I noticed a dozen or more people in tiger masks running through the circle with large Nerf squirt guns, soaking the villagers.

I saw Teddy and Mick round up a few as others jumped in cars and took off.

"What was that about?" Ava yelled.

"I don't know, but honestly, it felt pretty good." I shrugged my shoulders and grinned.

Ava burst out laughing. "It really did!"

"Oh boy," I said, holding up my phone. "Another meeting was just announced for tonight. Shocking."

"Aunt Fern is at it again!" Ava declared.

Chapter Eleven

I was tired, sweaty, and my feet felt like balloons. Typically, the shenanigans Ava and I caused at the meeting were done while sitting at a table with other townspeople. Tonight, I opted to lie on one of the sofas on the side of the room with my bare feet propped up on pillows, one of the Community Center fans pointed directly at me on high and a gallon freezer bag filled with ice and wrapped with a cold, wet, dishtowel sitting on my head. I'm sure this was not attractive by any means, but a pregnant gal has to do what she has to do to survive.

There was a ceiling light glaring in my eyes and I felt a migraine coming on from the heat of the day, so I reached into my huge tote and pulled out my oversized sunglasses, then resumed my therapeutic position on the couch. *Nice. Now I could shut my eyes and no one would know.*

"Child, have you gone completely insane?"

Grandma Opal said, slapping the side of my leg.

"Ow, I'm trying to relax," I barked back at my grandma. "You carry two of these around in ninety-degree weather for a day and tell me how you feel. I should be in my home in bed. It's not my fault our family is nuts and has to micromanage town goings-on."

"You millennials are so soft. When I was pregnant, we didn't have good options in fashion—just these humongous fabric tents with large, silly bows—very infantile. IF we were even allowed to work, we were treated poorly. And forget about the men helping out. Really. You have it easy."

While I'm sure she was right, I didn't care at this moment with a migraine looming. I mumbled something incoherent at her to get her to leave me alone and continued to zone out, barely listening as the meeting began.

"I'm taking this one," I heard Ava say from behind me and I sat up slightly and watched her prop her sepia, red-manicured feet up on the couch that sat at a ninety-degree angle from me.

I felt less weird with a second preggo lying on another couch.

Aunt Fern used her gavel to start the meeting and I heard some moans go through the crowd as she started. I think people were getting frustrated with impromptu alerts buzzing on their phones every other day.

"I'll make this fast, people. First thing on the agenda is that we did well with the yard sale today—

especially for how quickly this had to come together. Thanks to everyone who pitched in—especially Betsy for taking a lot of the burden off my nieces while they're pregnant—which seems to be...um...draining them." I heard her giggle and felt multiple eyes on me.

Normally, I'd turn red, but I was already from the heat of the day and too tired to care for once. I heard a chair scrape next to me and flopped my head to see my hunky, salt-and-pepper-haired hubby gaze down at me with those big brown eyes. I reached a hand to him.

"Sweaty," he said after taking my hand.

"I want to live in the shower when we get home," I said.

Aunt Fern gave impressive numbers on the cumulative amount the town made from today. She moved to the next item on the agenda, concerning the squirt gun incident and reminding the people of Leavensport to not respond in revenge.

Zed Zimmerman piped up. "That was uncalled for—Teddy, Mick—did you throw those punks in jail?"

My husband responded from next to me, "No, we didn't throw anyone in jail. It was some teens having some fun. I'm sure some of their parents are upset with the signs you guys put up earlier in the week and they're reacting."

"It's not our fault. They started it with the graffiti," Zander snapped.

I started to jump up, but my stomach betrayed me, so Mick helped give me a push up. "You don't see Leavensport teens behaving that way," I told them.

"Exactly," the Zimmerman brothers agreed in unison.

"No, you aren't catching her drift," Ava started. "You two are behaving like children. Even our teens aren't behaving that way—heck—why am I insulting the children of Leavensport—sorry guys and gals— even *they* aren't behaving like hooligans."

The men had nothing more to add.

"Enough, people," Mary, who was normally quiet as a mouse, yelled. "You're all upsetting Mirabelle."

I sat up and took my glasses off. Mirabelle was sitting next to her mom, crying, as Carlos and Mary worked to console her.

"I'm sorry, Mirabelle," I said, feeling horrible. "I'm cranky from being hot—it's not a good excuse, though."

"I wanted to make things better not worse and it don't work," she wailed, upset by our arguing and probably from the scene the teens made today.

Even the Zimmerman brothers couldn't stand to see one of our towns most beloved members in tears. "Hey, Mirabelle, Ava was right—we've been acting like hooligans," Zed said. "Please, don't cry— maybe we should get on board with your plan."

Aunt Fern spoke up. "Maybe we need to come

together as a town to form a truce. Do we even know where this problem started?"

"Was it Ralph's murder?" Ava asked.

"For us," Zed said, "it started with finding out the farmland was being bought up—then later we hear about this mall, transportation to and from the city and all of a sudden, we're not a small farm town anymore, we're part of the metropolitan life."

"It's like none of us had a say and most of us have lived here our entire lives—there are generations of our family before us and now it's all getting torn apart," Bradley said.

I was surprised to hear him get involved, seeing that he ran the town paper.

"Well, I'll talk to Fatin about a meeting with people from the city so we can find some common ground," Aunt Fern said. "But, I think the reason those kids tried to ruin our day had to do with the billboard sign being changed."

"What sign changed?" Ava asked.

"Someone crossed out the word 'love' in the billboard Delilah and the kids from Leavensport made and wrote 'hate' in its place—it may have sparked our little squirt gun attack today," Aunt Fern said. The room buzzed with mutters. "Okay. That's it for tonight. We're going forward with Day Two of the yard sale tomorrow and we have security set up, and Delilah and Mirabelle are changing the billboard back after the meeting. Thank you both for all your hard work."

My phone rang and I looked down, not recognizing the number. "Hello?" I asked, trying to sit up. Mick scrambled to help me. "Right—okay, no name, though?" I took a deep breath and blew it out frustrated. "Alright, thanks for trying."

Mick helped me stand and I rolled my ankle around to loosen it up before sticking my feet back in my sandals.

"What was that about?" Mick asked.

"I'll tell you in a minute." I looked past him, waving to get Aunt Fern's attention, then pointing to the kitchen, so she'd meet me there. Then I towed Ava into the kitchen by the wrist as Mick followed.

"What's up?" Ava pulled her arm away from me.

"I just got a call. I contacted the billboard company to see who paid for that initial sign that created friction. They just called back. It was paid through the mail in cash, no name."

"Well, that's just ridiculous. They have to have some sort of information to create an account," my Aunt Fern said.

"They had a P.O. box number from Leavensport with the name Robert Smith attached to it and cash—they said there was a business name of *Grendel's Mor*. Which you and I need to add to our slides to look up," I said to Ava.

"Grendel's Mor—what's Mor?" Aunt Fern asked.

We all shrugged.

"Grendel from Beowulf? Don't you remember senior English class?" I asked Ava.

"Oh yeah," Ava said. "I actually dug that story and I liked Grendel, too. It wasn't his fault his mother was horrid."

"Maybe Mor means mother," Mick said.

"Something for another day. Right now, I'm beat and want a cold shower and bed," I said, walking toward the door.

"Unfortunately, I'm not the reason for that," I heard Mick say to Ava and Aunt Fern.

"You kind of are the reason, if you really think about it." Ava laughed at her own joke.

I rolled my eyes and kept walking.

The next day, we were back out in the sweltering heat. Mick was kind enough to bring a cooler full of ice and cold water and slushies for both me and Ava. We were afraid the community yard sale traffic would die down today since there were issues yesterday, but it looked like more people showed up today than on Saturday.

My cell had been blowing up all morning with someone calling and hanging up on me. It rang again. I ignored it this time—there was no number—it read 'Private' on the screen.

"Still getting the hang-ups?" Ava asked.

"Yeah, at least I know not to answer it now."

"Do you think it has to do with what happened

to the mayor and Nancy—did we stumble onto something?" Ava asked.

"I don't know and this heat is making me cranky so I'm choosing to ignore it today." I slurped more of my cherry Slurpee Big Gulp then shoved it back into the cooler so it didn't melt immediately.

"Hey ladies, do you need to take a break and get in some air conditioning?" my mom asked with my grandma in tow.

"Oh, good Lord, yes," I said, taking my apron off and throwing it on the chair and doing the pregnant-woman-version-of-sprinting toward the Community Center.

Ava, carrying only one bowling ball in her stomach, was way ahead of me.

She was kind enough to wait at the door and we opened it to feel a blast of low humidity, cool air hit our skin. "I want to marry whoever created air conditioning."

"Me too," Ava agreed.

I paused momentarily to feel the dripping sweat evaporate. "Wow!" I moved toward the sofa, but stopped when I saw what looked like a heated conversation between some women I didn't know and my Aunt Fern. I moved closer as Ava followed.

"Is everything okay here?" I asked, squinting my eyes.

"Aren't you two the ones who meddle in all the crime in your town?" A big-haired red-head yelled at us.

"Whoa, you best be checking that tone, lady!" Ava's lower lip thrust out.

"Yes, do we know you?" I asked as politely as possible.

"Nope, but a lot of us have heard of you in the city. Seems your little town likes to make waves when it comes to the new mall," a shorter, spiky-haired lady said.

"Are we supposed to understand any of this?" Ava looked at Aunt Fern.

"I was trying to explain to these ladies that the people of Leavensport are all about finding a way to get along. No one here wishes them any harm, but they feel confident that small town politics are holding up the mall construction." Aunt Fern's tone was calming and diplomatic.

"Listen, you all are all upset about urban sprawl or some such nonsense and you've backed up the schedule," Beehive Redhead snarled.

"I don't think you're getting accurate information," I said, moving only my eyeballs to look at Aunt Fern.

"None of you know—but your *real* mayor knows what we're talking about." With that vague statement, the woman blustered off.

"What was that about?" I asked, watching the ice princesses storm off.

"I don't know, but I'd like to find out," Aunt Fern said with that bulldog look on her face I'd seen on my mom and my grandma before—and the one

Ava says I get sometimes, too—although, I don't believe her.

"Where are you going?" I asked after my aunt as she stomped off. "Where's she going?"

"Who knows—oh my!" Ava was looking down at her phone.

"Don't tell me Aunt Fern has already called another meeting." I reached for my cell to check it.

"No—it's not that. I took a picture of Luis Sanchez yesterday and sent it to Lolly—she just texted back." Ava turned her phone around showing me a picture of Luis.

"Yep, where'd you get that picture? He's in a sweater—no way was he wearing a sweater yesterday."

"That's not Luis—that's Theo when he was Luis's age." Ava looked at me intently.

"Whaaaat?" I held the word out as if it was six syllables. I could not believe the resemblance.

"Right? Yeah, that kid is related to the Sanchez family—no doubt about it."

"Did Lolly give you any information?" I asked.

"No, but it seems it's going to be time for me and my sis to have a heart-to-heart soon. I did tell her that we are having girls, too. I told her she better NOT tell mama and papa though."

"Okay, well, I guess we should go relieve my mom and grandma." I looked at my watch. "There's only another hour left before we shut down and I don't know about you, but I'm happy to shut down a little early."

As we were heading across the lawn to our booth, I saw my father sitting at a booth, having a coughing fit.

"Look who showed back up," Ava started to me. "Delilah's been coughing and pale lately too. Plus, she's been losing a lot of weight. I tried to get her to go to the doctor but she won't listen to me."

Ava kept walking as if she was ready to ignore my father, but I hung back and let her keep going to our booth.

"You had your number changed again," I said, standing over Chuck. "Are you sick?"

Chuck looked up at me with tears welled up in his eyes. I turned my head to the side and blew out a breath. It was getting more and more difficult to feel sorry for him the more he cried.

"Just a summer cold." He continued coughing, though, sounding like he was coughing up a lung. "I tried to call you several times today."

"Are you the one who was hanging up on me? Seriously?"

"I was nervous to talk to you—" he began.

"You wouldn't have to be nervous or cry all the time had you made a choice to be in my life. For some reason, you spent half of my childhood in Canada. You have a new phone number every few months—what are you involved in?" I demanded, hands on hips.

"I-I-I—" he stumbled as his body began to

shake and he looked around wildly.

I felt my entire body seize up as my ears prepared for a wailing shriek like an animal dying. This was the norm for us anytime I ever tried to confront him.

"Chuck." My mom walked up behind me, putting a hand on my lower back, then whispering to me, "You go on over to the booth and help Ava—there's a line."

Chuck's face lost all color as I turned and limped off, feeling all the energy drain from my body.

It was six o'clock, and I was home in my cozy air-conditioned living room, sitting with my feet up, two cats in my lap, and a bag of cookies and a glass of milk next to me. I was replaying *Big Brother* from last week, happy to not think about anything for once.

"Hey, babe, Lydia's here." Mick opened the door, momentarily emerging from his man cave.

"Oh, hey, where's Monty?" I asked as Lydia came in and grabbed a cookie from my bag and plopped in the chair next to the couch. I went to pause the TV.

"No don't, I haven't watched this episode. I want to see who got voted out and who won Head of Household," she said, taking a big bite of her chocolate chip cookie. "Oh yeah, the little guy's with his grandpa tonight."

"How's it going with your family?" I asked.

"It's going. I won't leave him alone with my mom. Funny, huh? My dad spent most of my life in jail and I trust him way more than my mom."

"It still amazes me that you and I hated each other all that time. We really have a lot of things in common—I mean—I trust my mom, but Chuck—no."

I took a breath and held my stomach and moaned.

"Are they kicking?" Lydia asked.

"Seriously, someone should warn pregnant women what's it's like to be pregnant," I said, shaking my head.

"There are a ton of books that do just that. Have you heard of a little book called *What to Expect When You're Expecting*?"

"Um, yeah—I just like to complain," I held the book up she was referencing. My mom bought it for me as soon as she found out.

Lydia laughed. "Well, at least we love each other now," she continued from my thought-process of us being nemeses since childhood.

"I mean, we tolerate each other now," I gritted my teeth and tilted my head before snickering.

"Right—we're fine—most of the time." Lydia looked off in space.

"True—except that one time you tried to steal Mick—but—"

"You know, maybe we should leave it at that."

Lydia laughed and I joined in as my phone rang.

"This better not be Chuck doing another hang-up." I looked down and saw it was my Aunt Fern and immediately rolled my eyes as I picked up. "Calling yet another meeting?" I grinned at Lydia, but then shushed her as I heard Aunt Fern say that my two uncles had started a brawl at Jenni's Diner.

"Wait, what?" I yelled as she explained that the guys were kicked out and continued the fight on the sidewalk, where Ava tried to break it up and was elbowed in the stomach, knocked down, and rushed to the hospital.

As I hung up the phone, the red I'd seen in dreams and weird visions with Donald Duck washed over my mind again.

Chapter Twelve

I felt like Godzilla stomping through the halls of the hospital to find my prey. I spotted the two with heads hung low as the women in my family ripped them a new one.

I pushed through the fray of insane Tucker women and used my baby bump to push into Uncle Eddie. "You better hope and pray that she and that baby are okay," I hissed. "You think you had to hide before—you'll need to go to the ends of the freaking world to get away from ME if anything happens to either of them."

I turned to Uncle Wylie. "And YOU—I'm *most* disappointed in you—I know you best because you weren't the coward who left the family. You know Ava and you've watched her grow up. She's family and how you could allow this crap to cause harm to her or that unborn little girl is completely beyond me." Tears spilled over my stormy eyes.

"Try to breathe, baby." My grandma put a hand

on me.

I whipped around on her. "And YOU are a huge reason why Uncle Eddie left to begin with! You with your anger and always having to be on someone's SIDE! It's like you can't be happy unless you have people in the family pitted against each other. AND you play favorites—WHO does that? I want you all to leave. RIGHT NOW! GET OUT!"

My grandma's face jerked back like I'd punched her. Usually, I'd immediately regret lashing out like that. Heck, I don't believe I'd ever spoken to her with such contempt before. But right now, I didn't care—all I cared about was that Ava and that baby were okay. I couldn't bear the thought—

A nurse rushed over, with security close behind. "You need to quiet down over here or leave," the nurse said curtly.

"Escort all of them out of here!" I looked at the guard and pointed to my stunned family.

"Jolie, Ava is awake and wants your family to come into the room—everyone." Delilah stood with crossed arms and puffy red cheeks.

"Are Ava and the baby okay?" I asked, rushing toward the room and brushing past Delilah to get to her. "I am SO sorry. I—I don't know what to say or to do." Panic starting sweeping through my entire body at the thought of something happening to the baby or her because of something my family did— our entire childhood flashed before my eyes. The thought of not having Ava in my life left me terrified.

"It's not your fault—it's their fault," she huffed, pointing at my two disgraced uncles, who stood in the doorway.

"Ava, you know I'd never do anything to hurt you in a million years—" my Uncle Wylie began.

"Yeah, we were completely wrong and out of line—and I'd give absolutely ANYTHING to take it back—are you and the baby okay?" Uncle Eddie's voice broke.

Ava sat quietly for a moment, looking from me to Uncle Wylie to Uncle Eddie to the women in my family who seemed to be holding their breath. For once, they were speechless and I'm sure it was from my rage moments ago.

"I want to say something first." Ava had an odd, determined look on her face that had me perplexed. "I've always felt like I was one of you— you all have always welcomed me with open arms— accepted who I was without fault and been my family when my own family left for the Dominican Republic. You've never missed a beat. I feel I've done the same for all of you."

"You have—" my grandma began, until Ava and I snapped our heads toward her with a look that commanded she be quiet.

"Today, I again tried to be a part of this family. When I saw you two men—who I consider to be my uncles—fighting, I thought about the pain you cause my best friend. The hours I've spent listening to her talk about her crazy dysfunctional family—why couldn't they just learn to get along? Why couldn't they let go? Why doesn't her dad love her? Why does he keep leaving? Why can't the rest of her family at the very least just be a cohesive family? And, I've been there. I've felt her pain—it became mine—because I love you all like family."

Mick had slipped into the room at the beginning of Ava's speech and moved behind me. I leaned back and rested my heavy body on him as tears dripped off of my cheeks.

"Then, I think about what happened tonight—I took an elbow in the gut—no—my baby—Ada—*she* took an elbow from people I called family. Delilah's been worried about me investigating crime going on in our little hamlet here—yet, it's those closest to me who are the biggest danger."

Ava stopped momentarily to compose herself. My bestie, who was my verbal sparring partner for life, was more serious than I'd ever seen her, and I felt as if I was standing on the edge of a cliff, waiting to be pushed over.

"So, with all that said—I'm fine. Little Ada, she's fine, too. She's got her mama's spunk and strength. But hear me when I tell you this—you two." She pointed at my uncles. "You two have a past and issues—and at least you're *trying* to work through it. You get points for that. And we all get why it's hard—everyone has baggage. So, you two figure your crap out—but until you do—you don't come near me or my child. Do you understand?"

My uncles looked at each other, then Ava, then

nodded. I could see the shame dripping from their skin.

I took Ava's hand. "If you can't come near her, then you best believe you won't be coming near me or my babies either."

I felt Ava squeeze my hand as we looked at each other.

My mom wordlessly pushed my aunt, my grandma, and the men out of the room. The moment they were gone, my emotional control crumbled. "Please don't hate me. I couldn't bear it—" I started, then a sob fell out and I sucked it back in.

"I could never hate you, girl. I don't hate them either, but they need to figure their stuff out. Maybe this will be the push they need."

Delilah walked up and held Ava's other hand. I looked at her, wondering if she was ready to thrash me. Instead, she looked at me knowingly, showing me that she understood the friendship that existed between her wife and me and that she respected it.

"I'm happy I'm a part of this family here," Mick said, wrapping his arms around me.

"We are too," Ava said, pulling her hand away from mine and patting one of Mick's hands that were resting on my midsection. "It's nice to have a guy in the mix to torture."

We all took a well-needed laugh.

"Hey," said Ava. "I was going to tell you earlier that Bea Seevers stopped me while I was helping

clean up and asked me about—of all things—
gambling chips, and if it were true a casino was
going to be built between Leavensport and Tri-
City."

My jaw dropped. "How could she know?"

"Well, she may just be the new Nancy—our
town gossip," Delilah said.

"But she's not in our group—would Devonte
tell her? He's the only one I've spoken to about the
chips outside of our group."

"Or we have a mole within our group.
Remember? I told you there was a mole within a
mole," Ava said.

"That makes no sense," I said.

"What doesn't make sense about it?"

"A mole within a mole—this isn't Russian
nesting dolls!" I rolled my eyes, grinning.

"Huh? Now YOU aren't making any sense!"
Ava belted out, becoming a tad annoyed with me.

"So, there's a mole in Leavensport—but there's
a mole within our group—so the Leavensport mole
is the mole in our group too?" I was so confused.

"No—I mean—maybe—nah, I mean a mole-
within-a-mole."

"A Russian nesting doll," I said.

"Okay—enough of the Laurel and Hardy
routine, you two," Mick said, dragging me out of the
room by the arm.

"Do *you* know what she's talking about?" I

asked him out of the side of my mouth, waving at Ava and Delilah as I was towed away.

"Don't get me involved in your antics, lady," he replied.

🥄

"Thanks for meeting me on short notice, Karl," I said to Lydia's father that afternoon as we sat at a table in Jenni's Diner.

"It's safe to say that anything you, your husband, your kids, your family EVER needs—as well as Ava's—I'll be there—no matter what!" he said, referring to the last twenty years he'd spent in jail for a crime he did not commit. Ava and I stumbled on some truths in the middle of a case and now Karl had a second chance with his daughter and his grandson.

"That's really nice. I mean, you could have chosen to be bitter about all those years you lost with Lydia and Lord knows you could have ratted Lory out...I'm not sure I'd have chosen the path you did." I shook my head, thinking maybe I related a bit more to my uncles' feud when comparing it to what Karl went through. Letting go of things made sense when we thought about other peoples' conflicts, but when it's our own—it's a different story.

"Don't get me wrong," Karl admitted. "Knowing what I know now about what she did—I just can't even deal with her most of the time."

I noticed his hands had clenched tightly into fists. I didn't blame him—his ex-wife had betrayed him in the worst way. Rather than turn her in, he attempted forgiveness for his daughter Lydia and his grandson Monty's sake.

"Listen, I met you here to ask you about Chuck."

"Your dad?" he asked, confused by me calling him by his first name.

"Yeah, didn't you go to Canada with him for vacation before Lydia and I were born?" I asked, remembering what I overheard my mom and her friend Gayle talking about before.

Karl's gaze turned into a hard stare for what felt like centuries. He burrowed his green eyes into my blue eyes and I wished I knew what was running through his mind. I could tell he was deciding whether or not to share something.

I waited.

"We did," he began carefully. "Your dad has definitely made a lot of mistakes in his life, but I don't think he's all bad."

"Wow, that was a diplomatic response." I felt like I was tiptoeing through a minefield with this conversation.

Again, Karl stared at me—this time I felt like he was looking inside me for answers, wondering if I could handle what he had to tell me.

"What is it, Karl?" I finally had the nerve to ask.

"Your father isn't all he seems to be. He struggled with learning as a kid—he got Scarlet

Fever and it affected his speech and that led to some bullying, which led to Chuck rebelling. He got into gambling outside of school. He's struggled with it off and on ever since—it's gotten him beaten within an inch of his life a few times."

I saw Karl's expression shift to concern when he saw my face, which I imagined was sagging as if I'd aged six decades. Up until that moment, I didn't think anything could shock me when it came to Chuck.

"Okay." I didn't know what else to say.

"Yeah, so sometimes we took off to get away from people who were after him. Other times he did some things for the people that he owed." Karl waited for my response.

"I see—" I stammered.

"He was always at a crossroads of whether to get out of your life completely to keep you safe or to be in it—but he never could decide."

I slowly nodded with that straight-lipped face the Tucker women were known to have.

"I hope you aren't trying to justify things for him, though." I pushed my tongue into my cheek, now taking on the role of starting deeply into Karl's eyes. "I get that he's always been your best friend. I do. I'd do anything for Ava. But regardless of the Scarlet Fever and everything else—he made choices. He needs to live with the consequences. Everyone has baggage—everyone is damaged goods to some extent and we all damage each other. Still, we all get to make our own decisions in life." I paused and shook my head. "So yeah, thank you for being honest with me. I'm going to leave now, try to process this."

I stood, looked numbly down at my phone, then back at Karl. "Hey," I said slowly. "Would you be willing to help me with something?"

"Of course—anything."

I sat back down to quickly run something by him, then walked out of Jenni's Diner and called Chuck, leaving a message that I wanted to speak to him face to face tomorrow morning at my restaurant at nine a.m.

My phone rang as soon as I clicked to hang up. "Yeah," I said, curtly expecting it to be him.

"Hey it's Ava—listen, Delilah just told me that she went back to the homeless shelter to take some art for them to hang up inside and she saw a huge house being built on the next lot over and a sign up near the homeless shelter that read "Milanos' Diamonds in the Rough Coming Soon," she seethed.

"Huh," I mumbled, feeling dead inside. I noticed Delilah's vehicle pulling into the drive.

"Jolie—you okay?" Ava asked on the other end.

"Yeah, I gotta go," I said, hanging up and moving outside toward Delilah. "Hey, Delilah."

She turned before getting into her VW Bug. "What's up?" She stumbled a bit, then knelt near her car door.

"Whoa, are you okay?" I tried to help her up.

"I'm—yeah—sorry, I've been feeling a bit dizzy on and off today. I was coughing a lot earlier. I'm hoping I'm not catching a summer cold."

Weird. That's what Chuck said earlier. "Should we leave your car and I can run you home?"

"I don't want to put you out," Delilah said.

"Come on, you know we're family now—here take my arm," I said, reaching for her.

"Okay, but listen," Delilah said, getting into the CR-V, "I wanted to drive out by the new mall before going home."

"What? Why?" I asked.

"You know, I don't want Ava to know, so I'm going to opt not to tell you so it doesn't put you in a bad position. If you don't want to drive me out there, then I'll take my car." She reached for the door.

"Nope, let's go," I said, putting the Honda into drive.

"Thank you. It's not that I don't trust you," Delilah began.

"I'm not upset. I get it. We've done this before and I appreciate you not putting me in the middle of the two of you. Mick and I have to continually work on boundaries."

"Yeah," Delilah giggled. "Ava fills me in."

"You know, I forget that everything isn't just Ava and me anymore," I mused. "She tells you everything, I tell Mick everything."

"I know. Mick and I joke that we need to start

going out just the two of us," Delilah said.

I laughed. "You both probably need some time to vent *about* the two of us."

I felt Delilah turn toward me in surprise. "You're super mellow—it's kind of freaking me out."

"Me too," I said, pulling onto the recently laid concrete that would eventually become the mall parking lot.

"Drive over toward the sign. I want to get my flashlight out and see what all it says."

I obliged and looked on as Delilah flashed her light around. I noticed movement off by the opening to the tunnels. "Hey, shine it over there." I pointed.

Delilah moved her light quickly and I caught a glimpse of a figure that I swore was Marissa being pulled behind a wall by one of the Zimmerman brothers. Those long beards were hard to miss. I wasn't sure if they were attacking her or trying to help her not be seen by us.

"Did you see that?" I gasped as I put the CR-V in reverse, then drive to pull closer to the structure of the building.

I put the SUV in park and jumped out. "Hello? Who's there?" I fumbled with my phone, searching for the flashlight and seeing Delilah jump out with her light.

She held it up and was pretty sure I saw a silhouette coming off the light hovering behind that brickwork.

"Whoa." I moved toward the wall, but suddenly, the light went out. I turned to see Delilah had collapsed to the ground and passed out.

Chapter Thirteen

Luckily, Delilah came to quickly. I helped her into the passenger seat and rushed to the hospital, driving through the ambulance drop off.

"Hi, she's been dizzy all day and she collapsed about ten minutes ago and briefly lost consciousness. She came back to quickly, though. She said she had been coughing a lot this morning."

They took her in and another nurse called me over to get her information for insurance.

"I need to call her wife and have her come here," I said, reaching for my cell.

"Ma'am, we need to get some basic information down first, okay?" the nurse said tersely.

"I SAID I NEED to call her wife first!"

"Whoa, Jolie—go sit over there." Bea Seevers flew in like a super hero, turning to the nurse, asking what happened and filling her in with as much information as she knew about Delilah.

I walked a few paces away, feeling like I was starting to lose it. I wanted to call Ava but I worried about her driving here. I stared at my phone as my mind swam with visions of Chuck, the Milanos, tunnels with people I didn't trust running down them, Tom Costello running an underground club where criminal activity took place, Karl in prison, Lydia pushing me down on the playground for saying she didn't have a dad either.

Someone shook my shoulder. "Jolie," Bea said, leaning over into my face. "Are you alright? Do you need a doctor, sweetie?"

"I need Ava here but I don't want her to drive," I said, back to numb again. "How'd you know to come?"

"First things first, I was already here checking on the mayor. Plus I needed to talk to Lydia about something. Then I heard you snarling at that poor nurse from all the way down the hall. As for Ava— okay—hold on—stay here." She walked away, pulling out her phone.

I watched her confident pacing while she bossed someone around.

"Okay, I called Baggie and he's going to pick Ava up to bring her here to you. I told him what I knew from the nurse and he will tell Ava. She's safe. Now, what's going in that head of yours?"

"How is it I grew up here thinking it was a safe place to live? It was a lie the whole time. Am I that naïve? Do I even deserve to be a mother?" *Am I in some sort of shock right now?* I wondered.

"Oh sweetie." She squeezed my shoulder. "Of course you deserve to be a mother. You ask me, no one deserves it more. I watched you grow up. You were always a cute kid, but on top of that, you also had a beautiful spirit inside you. It drew people to you. Your grandma and I used to joke how much you loved to hide in that room of yours and you'd be content to never talk to anyone but Ava—yet people sought you out."

I stared at her in a daze.

"I was never a kid person. You asked why Earl and I never had kids. I had other plans for my life. I'd never thought about being a mom. But I was always hanging out with Ellie and Opal, so I got to see a lot of you two. I loved watching you girls grow into strong, independent women. I'm going to love watching you two raise girls of your own."

"Did Tom really have an affair with Ellie Siler?" I asked abruptly. I didn't seem to care about censoring conversations anymore, or even if I was sounding crazy. I think if I wasn't so numb, I'd have questioned this more.

Bea nodded her head slowly.

"Who all knows this? Does Betsy know—did Wanda know?" I asked, referring to Tom's wife who had passed on years ago.

Bea shrugged her shoulders.

At that moment, Ava crashed through the door, rushing toward me.

"I'll take you to her," I said. "Has she seemed

sick for long?" I asked as we walked toward the room. Silence. Ava seemed to be ignoring me, hiding inside her headspace as I'd just been doing. "Ava!"

"What?" She stopped. "I've had it! Why is everything falling apart?" She raised her arms to the heavens, then started pacing. "Okay, listen, Jolie. There's some stuff I didn't tell you. I've been hush-hush about how I got pregnant—IVF—unknown sperm donor. And—I never told you this part, but—they thought it might not work with me, so Delilah tried as well. We burned through the savings we'd had from her taking over the art store and the gallery when her parents decided to retire." I grabbed her arm and redirected her frantic pacing toward Delilah's room. She paused when we reached the door. "Hold on, I'll tell you the rest in a second."

We both walked inside and Ava hurried to her wife's side.

"We're fine," Delilah said, looking at Ava longingly.

"We're?" I looked from Delilah to Ava.

"She's pregnant too," Ava said.

I'd gotten the full scoop on Ava and Delilah. Turned out Delilah was due just weeks after Ava and I were due. They'd both been hiding it, trying to wrap their heads around it all and wondering how they would tell everyone—what people would think—which, quite frankly, shocked me. They never seemed to worry about what anyone else thought before. I felt like there were things they weren't telling me.

I went to the waiting room where Bea sat waiting patiently, knitting something or other.

"You didn't have to stay and wait," I said, sitting next to her.

My phone buzzed and I looked down to see a text alert from Gemma. I opened it and read that she found out Mayor Morrison was in charge in 1992, when the first wave of gentrification started.

Thanks—I had forgotten you were looking that up, I texted back.

Peggy told me to tell you that she found out Bobby is talking to Mayor Cardinal about building a casino near the mall and possibly a horse race track.

Well, well—a casino—gambling chips—Chuck—Bobby Zane—Mayor Nalini—Nancy? My brain was spinning again.

Thank her for me. Anything else? I asked.

Yeah, supposedly the casino name is BGS—it's supposed to stand for something—but no one seems to know what. Lastly, Ava asked something about Olin Shuttleworth—the warden at the city prison? He's been warden going on thirty-seven years now.

Thanks. So, Olin was warden back in 1992 when everything started—he's still there now.

"Jolie," Ava said, walking toward me in the waiting room.

"Yeah," I looked up from my phone, seeing Bea still knitting next to me.

"My Papa just called. My family is at my house now."

Chapter Fourteen

I awoke the next morning to Mick bringing me breakfast in bed. There was a tray with a single red rose in a white vase, a plate of bacon, scrambled eggs, home fries, and toast with strawberry preserves, orange juice, and a cup of hot tea.

"Whoa, what did we do to deserve this?" I asked, propping my pillow up behind me and getting ready to chow down.

"Bea's concerned about you. I am too." He gave me a worried smile. "You aren't taking calls from your family—they are blowing up my cell every hour on the hour." He held up his phone.

My brain started to fuzz over again. "I'm going to eat, first, okay?" I went back into robotic mode.

I ate every bite off my plate and finished up the tea then looked at the time. I'd be meeting Chuck within the hour. I wanted to stop by Ava's first to check on Delilah and see what was up with the Martinez family.

"You ready to talk?" Mick asked, coming in to take my tray.

"Can't right now. I need to run to Ava's then do an errand before I go into work today." I got up, kissing him, then shuffled into the bathroom to hop in the shower.

A half hour later, I was knocking on Ava's door. It swung open and Sophia Martinez appeared, looking beautiful in her everyday heels, perfect makeup, long, thick, dark hair. Her soulful black eyes crinkled as she looked at my belly and reached to embrace me.

"Jolie, I'm so thrilled to see you. Look at you— you look terrific," she said, touching my stomach.

Thiago, Ava's father, walked toward me. He was shorter than his wife and bore an uncanny resemblance to Antonio Banderas. I saw Lolly and Theo and their kids in the other room. Ava looked less than thrilled and Delilah sat quietly. I knew Lolly and Theo had been having marital problems for quite some time now and I'm sure Ava did not want to deal with their drama.

"Did Ava tell you what happened with my uncles?" I asked. Mrs. Martinez still frightened me a bit. I loved her like a mom but when Ava and I used to act up, she'd pull our ears to get us to behave when we'd cross a line. It wasn't pleasant and I wouldn't put it past her to do it to us as adults.

"She did—we called Wylie and had a word. He gave us Eddie's number. No need to worry—we can work things out. Everyone is fine and that's all that matters. I can't believe you're having twins and now these two are expecting as well!" She sounded downright gleeful.

I guess they didn't hold out on telling Ava's family about Delilah. I wondered who else knew.

"Hey," Ava said, walking toward me. "Want some tea?"

"Nah, I just ate. I wanted to check in and see how Delilah is doing today and see your family. I have to meet someone in a bit."

Ava's parents moved back to the room where everyone else was.

"They're moving back," Ava said.

"Really!?" I said, a bit surprised.

"Yep, I tried to reason with them all last night, but now that they know everything, they made the decision. Papa is looking for work here this week and they want to move back as soon as possible."

"Do Delilah's parents know about her?" I asked.

"They do now. Turns out Bea contacted them as well. Last night wasn't pleasant. It was a big reason we weren't sure what to tell anyone. Her parents have never been thrilled with the idea of us—and before you get all worked up—it's not because we're gay—it's more about Bradley. He's been able to let go, but they worry about me with Delilah. When we told them I was pregnant, they seemed leery about it—so when Delilah found out she was pregnant—well, she wanted to keep it under wraps for at least the first few months."

"Well, seems like everyone knows everything now. You know the Milanos are moving back—construction already underway on their house and jewelry store," I said.

"I heard that. How is it we are such close friends and business partners, but the last few weeks I feel like I've barely been able to see or catch up with you?"

"I know—it may be part of the reason I've felt so off lately," I said, looking down at my watch. "Listen, I have to go. If you're tired from being up dealing with...or should I say Pudding Up with Relatives," I winked at her as she grinned at me, "then feel free to stay home and I'll get one my family to come fill in, or maybe Bea. Then I wouldn't have to ask my family."

"You need to speak to them at some point," Ava said.

"Yep, I'm off to do that now." I turned to leave.

Several minutes later, I parked and went into Jenni's Diner. I wondered if Chuck would bother to show. I prepared myself for either outcome.

"Jolie, over here," I heard him call from a back corner of the diner.

Jenni looked at me to see if I wanted tea, but I shook my head while holding up one hand.

"Good morning," I began, sitting down at the table and putting my hands together.

"Do you want to order? I'll buy us some breakfast," Chuck said.

"No thanks, this won't take long—" I started, but he cut me off in another coughing fit. "Are you alright?"

"I'm fine—what's up?" he asked, taking a napkin to cover his mouth as he coughed again. He pulled the napkin down and I saw blood in it.

"What's wrong?" I asked too calmly.

Chuck looked down to see the bloody napkin. His hands started to shake and more tears came. I felt nothing and sat waiting for him to tell me what was going on. When he finally calmed his emotions down, he seemed to study my expression.

"Are you okay?"

"That's what I asked you. I'm waiting for you to answer," I simply stated.

"Daddy's got lung cancer," he said. He let out a quiet wail.

I felt my body cringe hearing him use the word 'Daddy.' I think he took the cringe to mean I cared.

"You're Chuck to me—not Daddy. I'm pregnant, and married. I'm dealing with my family—my husband, my kids, my friends, my family—the Tucker family—you, well, I'm sorry you're sick. I'm sorry you got Scarlet Fever in school and were bullied. I'm sorry you got involved in gambling and did some—" I stopped searching for the right word.

"How'd you know all that?" he spat out, taking

a new tone.

"What's it matter? You lied. So what? Seriously, so—what? It's not the worst thing you've put me through all these years. What I came here to tell you is that you will not be a part of these babies' lives. They won't know what it is to have someone there just to leave on any whim and not show up for years." I stood and reached down for the glass of ice water and slowly took a few gulps before turning around and leaving.

I had called Bea Seevers and asked if she'd be willing to go in and take some orders this afternoon so I could take care of some family business. She'd been a godsend to me lately. Next, I called Ryder and he was willing to go in and cook.

I contacted everyone in my family through group chat text and asked them all to meet me at my house at noon.

Everyone came in quietly and gathered around the large wooden table that overlooked the woods outside the sliding glass door. I'd set glasses out and made both iced tea and lemonade and had pitchers of each on the table. I held my hands out, indicating for my guests to serve themselves.

Uncle Eddie was there with his wife, Shelly, and their adult kids—my cousins. They looked mortified sitting across from Uncle Wylie.

"So, everyone here knows what's going on with Aunt Shelly, Uncle Eddie, and Uncle Wylie," I leapt into my speech. "I don't know how any of it gets fixed—but listen—either fix it or decide not to and move on—or don't—you can choose to continue being angry, bitter, and nasty for years to come— battle each other until the day you all die—just know this," I held a breath in then let it out, taking a moment to think if I truly meant what I was about to say. "If any of you decide to do anything other than moving on and letting go, then you won't be in my life or in the twins' lives." I stood up straight, feeling rooted to the hardwood floor beneath me.

"She's right, you all know it," Tink spoke up first.

"That's not difficult for you to say," Karly said to Tink. "You weren't lied to and kept away from your dad for your entire childhood."

Tink—or Eddie Jr, Sadie, and Serenity were all the kids of Eddie and Shelly. Kevin and Karly were Shelly's kids—and my Uncle Wylie's. Eddie and Shelly knew this but it was news to everyone else as of the last year.

My Uncle Wylie nodded toward his brother. "I can try to let it all go if you and Shelly are willing to allow me to get to know Kevin and Karly," he shifted his gaze to them, "—I mean—as long as the two of you want to get to know me."

Grandma Opal started to speak up but mom and Aunt Fern shushed her.

"I want to know you," Kevin said, looking at his dad.

I saw Uncle Wylie's shoulders relax a little. "Karly?" he asked, looking at her.

Karly looked at my Uncle Eddie and her mom, Shelly, first. Both sat stone faced and silent.

"I'd like to get to know you, too. I don't want to hate—" She stopped looking at my Uncle Eddie trying to think of the right word to call him.

"He raised you, Karly. You can still call him Dad," Wylie said.

Karly stared at him, then at Eddie, who pushed the chair out and stood, walking around the table to stand over his brother.

I could see the dimple in Wylie's cheek twitching as he looked up at him.

"Truce, little brother?" Eddie held out a hand.

Uncle Wylie looked at his brother's hand for a long time, then looked over at Kevin and Karly and reached up to hug Uncle Eddie.

I released a huge breath I hadn't realized I'd been holding in and poured myself some iced tea.

Chapter Fifteen

"So, you were the one to end the Tucker family feud." Ava wiped her mouth from the fruit cobbler I'd made us earlier that evening. She'd come over so we could catch up on everything from the last couple of weeks.

"I hope it sticks." I opted to not talk to anyone about my most recent conversation with Chuck yet.

I filled Ava in on the text the Gemma had sent me and other things I'd found out, including the information Karl gave me on Chuck's past.

"So, it seems Bobby Zane was trying to position himself as mayor here—do you think that ties into Mayor Nalini being shot?"

"I think it's pretty likely," I said, reaching for my cell.

"Who are you calling?" Ava asked.

"Why, the man himself. Bobby Zane," I said, while texting Betsy to see if she had his number.

"Wait, is that a good idea?" Ava asked.

I shrugged my shoulders, lifting my tea cup for another swig of coconut chai. Betsy texted back almost immediately and I clicked the number to dial.

"Hello?" Bobby answered on the first ring.

"Mr. Zane, this is Jolie Tucker. How are you doing this evening?"

"I'm fine, what's this about?" he asked.

"I'd like you to come for a visit. Are you busy right now?" I watched Ava's jaw drop. I put a finger to my lips to try and keep her quiet.

"Well, I'm not sure I can just pick up and leave right—" Bobby stopped, and it sounded like he covered the mouth piece and was talking to someone. "Okay—you know—yeah, just give me your address and I'll be right over."

I obliged, giving him my address and then began picking up after Ava and me.

"What are you doing?" Ava asked, following me around the room.

"You're going to hide in that closet there while recording our conversation. Now, go in there and hit record—I'm going to talk in the kitchen, the dining room, and in the living room so we can test if it will record in all places in case he moves around while we talk." I pointed to the coat closet off the living room.

I looked around, making sure there was no other evidence that Ava or anyone else had been here. I put the cups and plates in the dishwasher and wrapped up the cobbler to put back in the fridge.

"Jolie—you can't be serious," Ava protested. "This guy is dangerous. You're inviting him into your home."

I pointed to the closet, staring at her. She reluctantly turned to go with her phone in hand and I heard her grumbling as she pushed the coats aside to make room, then a muffled-sounding "Ready!" came from the closet.

I stood in the kitchen and in a normal, conversational tone said, "Pudding Up with Relatives." Then I did it again in the dining area and again in the living room. "Okay, come on out."

She played back the recording—the phrase in the kitchen could barely be heard, but the living room was perfect. The dining room was something we could make out, but it was iffy.

"Why don't you record on your phone?" Ava asked.

"I want him to use my phone at some point. I could keep your phone under the couch pillow on record," I said, moving the pillow away to see if that would be noticeable. I put a blanket over it.

"Then why don't you let me be here with you? He's less likely to do anything with both of us in the room," Ava said as I rooted around in her purse. "What are you doing?"

"I'm moving your car to the barn for now," I

said, rushing out to move Ava's car. I came back in and she was still staring at me like I'd lost my mind.

"If you hear me say 'gliding through a minefield,' then you can come out," I said, pushing her inside the closet and reminding her to shush.

Several minutes later, there was a knock on the door. I opened it and invited Bobby inside. He had on Dockers, beige shorts, boating shoes with no socks, and a Leavensport Lions T-shirt. He came in and I offered him a seat on the couch, which he took immediately.

"Would you like anything to drink? Coffee, tea, soda?"

"Maybe a cup of coffee, if you have some made. Boy, it's chilly in here," he said, rubbing his arms.

"Oh yeah, sorry—being pregnant I'm hot all the time. I think I've been freezing Mick out of the house lately," I said, pouring a cup of coffee and handing it to him, then filling a small pot with hot water, a cup, and a tea bag and bringing it to the couch for myself.

"Is your husband here?" Bobby asked.

"Nope, he's working—probably still trying to figure out who shot and killed Nancy and tried to kill the mayor." I poured a little water into the cup with the teabag, added a little Sweet'N Low then took a sip.

"I heard he's going to pull through." Bobby shifted on the cushion.

"Looks that way," I said, taking another sip.

Bobby cupped his hands around his coffee to warm them up. "So, why'd you invite me here?"

"Well, you know, I think you may have gotten yourself tied up in a situation that you can't seem to get yourself out of and I'd like to help you with that." I set my tea cup back onto the saucer and leaned back in my chair.

Bobby's eyes darted around the room and he began fidgeting with both hands.

"I'm not working for them," I said calmly. "My biological father got caught up in something similar back in the day—for all I know, it's with the same group you're mixed up with—but I'd like to offer you an out."

"I—I don't know what you're talking about." Bobby stood up and began pacing, then moved to the dining room.

I looked at the pillow where the phone was hidden and recording.

"Come here. I want you to hear for yourself from Mick," I said, using my right hand to coax him over near me.

Bobby reluctantly walked over to the chair where I sat.

I dialed Karl's number, counting on him to play the part of Mick on speakerphone like we'd planned.

"Hey, sweets," Karl said on cue.

"Hey babe, I wanted you to know that Bobby is

here now and I talked to him a little about offering him an out from whatever he's mixed up in," I said into the phone.

Bobby eyed me suspiciously then said, "I've never said I'm involved in anything."

"Listen, man, we can put you in protective custody if you'd be willing to give us the names of who is putting the squeeze on you," Karl said, still pretending to be Mick.

Bobby's eyes darted around the room again. I noticed his arms and neck start to get blotchy and wondered if he was like me in that when he got nervous, he broke out in rashes. He started itching his arms. He looked down and saw the blotches, then grabbed the blanket to pull over his legs, knocking the pillow off the couch, and Ava's phone was exposed.

I thought I'd been on a winning streak with the straightforward talk the last few days. I had success with Karl, Chuck, and my family—I figured this would work, too. I guess I was wrong.

"What's this—are you setting me up?" Bobby looked at Ava's phone, then around the house again, like he was expecting someone to come busting out of a room.

"We're trying to help you—give you a way out," I said, scooching to the edge of the chair and putting a pillow protectively over my stomach. I'd thought if I could get Bobby to give us the names of who was threatening him, then I could work out a deal with Teddy, Mick, and Tabitha that Bobby could testify against Jackson Nestle—the man I assumed was behind all this, or at least mostly. Then Nestle could lead us to the Leavensport mole.

"I don't know who to believe anymore," Bobby said, reaching for the phone he had uncovered. He'd forgotten Karl was still on my speaker phone, overhearing everything as a witness too.

I reached for it at the same time and got it first, pulling it behind my back. "I swear I really am trying to help you," I said firmly. "You can testify against whoever it is—you can be protected."

"You don't understand what you've done!" Bobby started sweating, in spite of saying he was freezing earlier. "If they find out I flipped on them—nuh-uh, no way." Bobby started to walk toward the door.

"Wait!" I yelled after him.

Bobby was fiddling around, trying to yank his keys out of his pocket to get away from me as fast as possible when Ava came barreling out of the closet with a shovel in her hand. She grunted and swung the shovel, hitting him over the head.

Bobby fell to the floor with a loud thud.

"I never gave the code phrase—what did you do that for?" I yelled.

"It sounded like he was trying to attack you! He could have hurt you! If he killed Nancy, then what makes you think he wouldn't try to kill you?"

"This guy is too terrified to kill anyone," I said. "I need to call for an ambulance."

The front door swung open. "I'll take that." An older man stood there, leveling a gun at us. He had bright blue eyes with grayish eyebrows that were overgrown and bushy. White hair was slicked back and the wrinkles under his eyes made him look hard and mean.

I recognized him, but I couldn't place from where. He wasn't a resident of the village.

"Who are you?" Ava asked.

"None of your concern, now both of you get over there on the couch," he said, striding in and shutting the door.

I glanced at the screen of Ava's phone to make sure it was still recording and pushed it between the cushions on the couch as I sat down.

"Nope, I'm not sitting down. I'm cramping and I need to stand." Ava held her stomach and looked at me.

I thought back to last spring when she faked cramps with a guard at the homeless shelter to give me time to get inside and find out some information.

"Here's the thing, lady, I don't care," he yelled, jamming the barrel of his gun into her back. "You and those unborn fetuses aren't going to be around for much longer anyway—so sit down!"

Ava yelped in pain and fell to the couch. I reached for her, but he held the gun up, threatening to pistol whip me. Ava was bent over in pain but waved at me to stop, so I backed off, putting my hands up in the air.

I felt my body begin to quiver all over and knew I had bitten off way more than I could chew with this plan. I tried to place where I'd seen this guy before.

The man pulled his phone from his back pocket and read the screen. It must have been a text because he glanced up at us as he sat down in the chair I'd just sat in while talking to Bobby, who was still splayed out on my floor. The man laid the gun down on the arm rest, eyeballed Ava and me, then looked at our very pregnant stomachs and finally back down to reply to the text.

Ava was sitting closest to the gun. I saw her shift her body toward it. I shook my head at discreetly as I could. *Don't do it, you pregnant idiot!* I screamed inside my head.

"I wouldn't do that if I were you," the man said, reading her mind. Ava slumped back, defeated.

"What do you want with us?" she asked.

"Just a minute—and sent. Okay—what do I want with two country bumpkins? Absolutely nothing. Killing you two will make a lot of people very happy," the man said, standing and towering over us. "Besides, who do you think shot that Nancy bird? She tried to lean on the wrong guy. Now she's dead. And I did your entire town a favor with that Mayor Nalini or Falini—not only was he a witness but an easy way to grab some power."

"You bastard!" growled Ava. "Who are you, anyway? I've never seen you before in my life!"

The man chuckled grimly. "Oh, my dear, I have been around for a very long time. I'm Olin Shuttleworth. I would say I'm pleased to meet you, but..." He shrugged.

I knew I'd seen him and someone told me his name—I just hadn't been putting the two together.

Behind him, I saw the front doorknob turn and open a tiny bit and my heart sank to the ground, thinking it was Mick getting home from work. I didn't want this man to shoot my husband.

Ava glanced that direction as well. She suddenly seemed determined to draw the attention to herself. "Country bumpkins—who you calling a bumpkin, you old geezer?"

The man's lip curled a smidge as he looked down at Ava. "You'll be first." He pointed the gun toward my friend's head.

"Good, it will give Jolie more time to figure out how to handle you." She crossed her arms pushing her head against the barrel.

"Ava!" I yelped.

I couldn't believe it when Earl and Bea Seevers came through the door, inching quietly toward the man with the gun at Ava's head. I pleaded with my eyes for them to not do anything.

Bea reached down carefully, carefully picking up a jingle ball that our cats played with. Then she threw it into the dining room, causing the man with the gun to jerk his head up and move his gun hand. At that second, I threw myself at Ava and jammed her body into the couch, covering her. "Stay down," I whispered and held my head up to see if the Seeverses would be okay.

Mrs. Seevers drew back a whip she had in one hand and cracked it in the air. It wrapped multiple times around the wrist of the man's gun hand. She pulled back hard as the weapon fell. Simultaneously, Mr. Seevers took a red robe tie and put it around the man's neck and began pulling. Bea grabbed the gun from the floor.

"I got it, Earl. I got the gun!" Bea yelled.

I rolled off of Ava and asked if she was okay as I worked to push myself up off the couch then help Ava up. I was still shocked by the superhero routine I'd just witnessed from this sixty-something-year-old couple.

Mr. Seevers released the man's neck and took the gun from his wife, aiming it at the man.

"How did you two know to come here?" I had known these people since birth and found myself completely flabbergasted by their behavior twice in the last month.

"Earl saw Olin in town and stopped for a chat. He told Earl he was there to visit *you*. He said that you two were old friends and he was going out to your house," Mrs. Seevers said. "But I remembered that you had no clue who he was and I had to tell you. I knew something was off, so I told Earl we'd best come on over to make sure everything was okay."

"Okay, that's it. Let's make this official—you

and Earl are official Tuckers and Martinezes," Ava said, reaching out to hug her.

"You saved all of us!" I reached for Bea's hand and put it on my stomach as Ava nodded in approval, putting her hand on the little one growing inside her.

I heard sirens wailing in the background as Karl, Lydia's dad, came running in. "Are you all okay? I'm so sorry—I had a flat tire. I tried to drive on it but it was sparking so bad—so I stopped, called the police, and flagged down a ride from this gentleman." He jerked his thumb behind him, and Jackson Nestle walked through the door. I glared at him, and then the realization struck me. I had never hung up on Karl! He had been on the phone the entire time.

Nestle walked over, looking down at Bobby Zane, who was beginning to moan and wake up. "Pathetic. Beaten by a bunch of pregnant girls," he muttered in disgust. Then he looked hard at the gunman, who was still down on his knees from the beating the Seeverses had given him.

Mick came running in the door, then immediately recoiled after observing his surroundings. "What's going on here—are you two alright? There's an ambulance pulling in here now."

Chapter Sixteen

Several days later, I sat out on our deck overlooking the woods with my journal and a huge Mason jar of iced tea, waiting for Mick to get home from work so we could enjoy the pot roast I had in the Dutch oven. I needed to get a grasp on everything I'd learned the last few days.

Ava and I were checked out by a doctor and determined that we and the babies are okay. We'd called Delilah and my family to let them know what had gone down at the house and that we were fine. On doctor's orders, we rested that night in the hospital under observation, but then went home the next day. Ava came over to my house so she and I could add everything to our I Spy Slides while it was all fresh in our minds. However, our debriefing session was interrupted every half hour or so by visitors, all scrutinizing us for lingering damage.

Aunt Fern is happy to give the mayoral duties back to Mayor Nalini soon. He is making huge strides in recovery and the doctor's anticipated he'll be out of the hospital and finished with his speech therapy sessions by September.

They arrested Bobby and tried to hold him based on the recording—that he knew and withheld information. They questioned him, kept him for seventy-two hours, but in the end, some big shot mafia attorney named Coco Ragino got him out. Mick knew of that attorney from growing up with his mafia family and knew Bobby must somehow be connected more than he was letting on if Coco Ragino was involved. Bobby could have easily filed charges against Ava for whacking him with the shovel, but apparently, he decided not to push his luck with the Leavensport legal system at this juncture.

Turns out good ole Nancy was an excellent gossip even from beyond the grave. She'd been smart enough to know that blackmailing these people could be trouble, so she'd mailed a letter to Mayor Nalini explaining everything she knew— which turned out to be very little, but still enough to let us all know we were onto something. Problem was, since Lahiri, who lived with Mayor Nalini, was so overwhelmed with everything that was happening, she neglected to sort through the mayor's incoming mail. It was all thrown in a basket. Nancy couldn't have known they'd come for her, let alone that the mayor would end up in the crosshairs.

In her letter, Nancy revealed that she had

accidentally overheard a conversation the warden, Olin, had with Bobby Zane. She heard Olin threaten to harm Bobby's parents if he didn't follow orders. He wanted Bobby to weasel his way into politics here in Leavensport to get a bill passed to zone for a casino.

Nancy went on to explain in her letter that she had been having some financial problems and had gone to Tri-City to get in on a Texas Holdem tournament, hoping for a lucky break. Unfortunately, she'd lost even more money. Finally, out of desperation, she tried to use the information she'd heard to blackmail the warden.

The information in the letter filled in a lot of pieces of the puzzle, and what Bobby told the police cleared up the rest. I don't think Nancy had bargained for how crooked the guy she was trying to blackmail was. He had gotten wind of Nancy and the mayor's meeting and decided to put a stop to it. He'd grabbed Bobby after he left Chocolate Capers and threatened to kill him and his parents, then took him to the B&B where Nancy and the mayor were meeting and told him to...take care of things.

After he was arrested, Bobby didn't want to talk, but eventually told the police that he had been under duress, and that in the end, he couldn't go through with the hit. He'd gotten cold feet outside the B&B and started arguing with Olin. He threw his coffee drink into the warden's face to blind him, then jumped behind some bushes and hightailed it out of there. He never thought the warden would be

*crazy enough to shoot anyone himself—Bobby
seemed to think Shuttleworth was a guy who didn't
want to get his hands dirty—or at least that's what
he told the police. Then I guess he laid low for a day
or two. That explained the cup from Betsy's being
left at the crime scene.*

*According to what the mayor had been able to
communicate so far, when Olin had burst into the
conference room at the B&B, Nancy had been trying
to fill him in on what she knew about Olin
Shuttleworth. According to her letter, she'd written
the letter because when she had called the mayor the
day before, Lahiri had answered the phone and said
her uncle had been called to an emergency
meeting—something to do with land being bought
near the Villy Crisis Center. That didn't sit right
with Nancy, so she sent the letter to cover all of her
bases. And it was a good thing she did.*

I had stopped writing briefly to think back to
when Noah Morrison ended up dead. "Huh," I said
aloud.

"Rrrrreeow?" asked Bobbi Jo.

"I don't understand organized crime," I said,
petting her pretty head. "Noah Morrison follows
orders and then gets bumped off in prison.
Meanwhile, Bobby fingers the warden of Tri-City
Correctional Institution for murder, and he gets a
mafia attorney. Does that make sense to you,
kittums?"

Bobbi Jo flopped over on her back, demanding
tummy scratches.

"You're right. I should add that to our I Spy Slides," I agreed, rumpling her soft belly.

Later that night, Mick and I were sitting at the table when the doorbell rang. Ava appeared, holding the pregnancy book we were going to read together—the one Lydia told me about, the one everyone on Earth had heard of except Ava and me. Of course, we had her stay for dinner.

"So, how did Bea's robe tie get there?" I asked Mick once Ava had gotten settled at the table. I had been itching to debrief him now that he had finished questioning everyone.

"Mr. Seevers told me that those two do their funny business not just at home—they like to get a room at the B&B too every so often."

That's weird, I thought. *Bea said they had never gotten a room there. Maybe she thought it would make her a suspect? Or maybe she was embarrassed?* I made a mental note to add that to I Spy Slides to look into later.

"Well, I'm happy those two are so kinky—saved our butts that night," Ava said, chewing.

I couldn't argue with that.

"And Ryder?" I asked, referring to the paint can that was found at the shooting.

"Yes," Ava said simply.

"Huh?" I asked.

"Oh, the answer to your earlier question is yes. It *was* all a coincidence. Ryder isn't only a surfer—he's a surfer with psoriasis—which is why he wears long sleeves and hoodies so much—but he's also an artist and the hospital has commissioned him to create a mural on the roof with a large heart for their Heart Smart Campaign coming up. That's what you saw—him going up to paint with his duffel bag of spray paint, his art supplies—the B&B hired him to make them a mural too—I guess he dropped a spray paint can—so that explains that clue that was at the scene."

"But wait." My head was spinning. "Why did he run? At the hospital? He tore out of there like...well, like he was afraid of getting caught!"

"That was when Carlos had to leave suddenly because of the construction issue. I called Ryder and he told me he could be there in five minutes. He made it in four." Ava stared at me. "So, yes it was all a coincidence and..." She waited.

"And what?" I crossed my arms.

"You know," Ava drew out the words.

"Oh, you want me to admit I was wrong."

I saw Mick grin, then turn his head in the hopes I hadn't seen. He studied his fork, then rearranged his napkin to avoid looking at me.

"Okay fine, for ONCE, you were right and I was wrong," I said, biting my lip. Then my head snapped up. "Wait. He already had the hospital gig when he talked to Delilah about being a painter. Why didn't he tell her that the hospital hired him to paint that mural then?"

Mick and Ava looked at each other and

shrugged. "Maybe he was trying to hedge his bets with getting a job," Ava suggested. "You know, since you seemed determined to NOT hire him for so long. Man's gotta eat, ya know? And he probably thought if you knew he was also looking elsewhere, you'd be even less likely to hire him."

I glared at her. She was extremely good at making me feel like a total jerk. But that did make sense.

I hadn't had time to revisit what Mayor Nalini had said about my Aunt Fern being in danger. I wanted to ask Mick about it, but I feared his family could be involved. I had chewed him out for not being honest with me about Imelda earlier, and here I wasn't sure he'd choose me and my family over his. Another thing I couldn't get out of my head was when I thought I saw Marissa and a Zimmerman brother at the mall the night I drove there with Delilah. I'd seen Marissa since then and she seemed fine, which led me to believe that she and the Zimmermans were working together and up to no good. I rubbed my stomach, thinking about the third and final trimester of this pregnancy approaching. I'd had a naïve notion that Ava and I would have this entire village's history of crime figured out by the birth of our babies—now I wasn't so sure.

Recipes

Hoisin and Boyzin Glazed Pork Chops

Ingredients:

- 4 Pork chops, boneless (about 2 lbs)
- 3/4 tsp Salt
- 2 tbsp Sesame oil
- 2 Garlic cloves, minced
- 2 tsp Ginger, minced
- ⅓ cup Hoisin sauce
- 2 tbsp Rice vinegar
- 2 tbsp Water

Directions:

1. In a small saucepan set over medium heat, simmer the garlic, ginger, Hoisin, rice vinegar and water, whisking occasionally until the mixture is fully combined, about 4 minutes. Set aside.
2. Lightly salt pork chops. Heat the sesame oil in a large skillet over high heat. Once oil is smoking, place the pork chops in the skillet, cook without turning until well browned, 4-6 minutes on each side (adjust timing based on how thick your pork chop is). When a thermometer is inserted into the thickest part registers 135°F, remove the pork chops from the pan. Transfer to a cutting board and let rest 5 minutes.

   ***Serve with Hoisin sauce drizzled over top!

   ***Add a coleslaw to add extra crunch—lots of great Asian slaw recipes out there!

Cast Iron Cashew Chicken Noodle

Ingredients:

- 8 ounces uncooked thick rice noodles
- 1/4 cup reduced-sodium soy sauce
- 2 tablespoons cornstarch
- 3 garlic cloves, minced
- 1 pound boneless skinless chicken breasts, cubed
- 1 tablespoon peanut oil
- 1 tablespoon sesame oil
- 6 green onions, cut into 2-inch pieces
- 1 cup unsalted cashews
- 2 tablespoons sweet chili sauce
- Toasted sesame seeds, optional

Directions:

Cook rice noodles according to package directions.

1. Meanwhile, in a small bowl, combine the soy sauce, cornstarch and garlic. Add chicken. In a large cast-iron or other heavy skillet, sauté chicken mixture in peanut and sesame oils until no longer pink. Add onions; cook 1 minute longer.
2. Drain noodles; stir into skillet. Add cashews and chili sauce and heat through. If desired, top with toasted sesame seeds.

Pudding Up With Relations Iron Skillet Hot Fudge Pudding Cake

Ingredients:

- 1-1/4 cup sugar divided.
- 7 Tablespoons cocoa divided.
- 1/4 teaspoon salt
- 1 cup flour
- 2 teaspoons baking powder
- 1/3 cup butter melted.
- 1/2 cup milk
- 1/2 cup brown sugar
- 1-1/2 teaspoons vanilla
- 1-1/4 cup hot water

Directions:

1. Combine 3/4 cup sugar, flour, 3 Tablespoons cocoa, baking powder and salt.
2. Blend in milk, butter and vanilla. Beat until smooth.
3. Pour batter into oiled 10-inch iron skillet.
4. Combine remaining sugar, brown sugar, 4 Tablespoons cocoa and sprinkle over batter.
5. Pour hot water on top.
6. Bake at 350 degrees for 30-35 minutes.

Let stand 15 minutes before serving. If desired, top with whipped cream and/or ice cream.

Summer Fruit Skillet Cobbler

Ingredients:

- 5 cups assorted fruit
- 1 teaspoon vanilla
- 1 teaspoon ground cardamom (Oddly enough, I don't like cardamom, but I do like ginger—so I switch this to ginger).
- 1 tablespoon brown sugar
- 1 teaspoon chopped fresh rosemary (Personally, I leave this out—not a fan.)
- ½ cup whole wheat flour
- ½ cup all-purpose flour
- ½ cup old-fashioned oats
- 2 tablespoons hemp seeds (I've never been able to find these in a store so I substitute sunflower seeds and I've used pistachios ground up).
- ¼ cup brown sugar
- 1 ½ teaspoons baking powder
- Pinch salt
- 1 teaspoon chopped fresh rosemary (again, I leave this out)
- 2 tablespoons margarine
- ¾ cup milk, plain

Directions:

1. Stir fruit, vanilla, cardamom, brown sugar, and rosemary together in the bottom of a 9-inch cast iron skillet.
2. In a medium bowl, mix together flours, oats, hemp (sunflower or pistachios ground) seeds, brown

sugar, baking powder, salt, and rosemary. Cut in margarine with a fork. Mix in milk until smooth.

3. Pour spoonfuls of cobbler dough over the fruit.

4. Bake at 375 degrees F for 35-40 minutes.

Serve warm.

Makes 8 servings

From the Author

This book was a ton of fun to write. I always say that, though. Why? Because I'm a HUGE research geek. This time, I got to research Beijing, China and our new surfer/expert in Asian cuisine/handsome-James Dean-bad boy who occasionally deals with bouts of psoriasis, Ryder Chen. Maybe that seems like an odd combination: a handsome James Dean who also deals with psoriasis—but hey—in reality, even the insanely hot guys and girls out here deal with real issues and have insecurities and flaws. For example, did you know that James Dean was in a MAJOR accident that knocked out some of his teeth and many of them were fake? It's true! Also, Mr. Cool himself—his first official gig was a soda commercial. So see, everyone has external and internal flaws and I want my readers to really connect with my characters!

This time around, my list of research topics was quite diverse. Here's a peek at my list:

- Burner phones
- Physical signs of cancer
- Chinese Proverbs
- James Dean
- Coma
- Diversity
- Graffiti
- Mafia—organized crime in Sweden as one of many subtopics!

- Pregnancy—second trimester
- Psoriasis
- Surfer slang
- Types of signs—meaning commercial signs
- Effective communication
- Journaling
- Therapy sessions
- Couple's therapy
- MS
- Writing comedy scenes
- Construction—building a mall
- Village politics
- Gentrification
- Urban Sprawl

That's a quick taste of the research topics that go into each book that I write. I spend a lot of time in libraries, book stores, interviewing people, driving around to take pictures of things that I need to visualize for scenes, and continually studying the craft of writing.

As always, if you find any mistakes in content, those are solely mine. If you'd like to share any with me, please email me at jrath@columbus.rr.com. I'm a life-long learner and I NEVER believe I'm right—I make mistakes ALL THE TIME—it's this thing called humanity I live with daily. LOL! So, if you find a mistake—let me know—I love to learn!

Punkin Strudel Mayhem Blurb

You know what they say: you are what you eat, and Jolie and Ava are about to turn into everything they have been craving, including pounds of chocolate, pizza, pickles, and ice cream.

After facing the mafia, urban sprawl, gentrification, and newborn babies, the lives of the Leavensport villagers will be altered forever. Change is inevitable. Jolie Tucker is a Type-A perfectionist with fanatic tendencies who detests the very thought of change. Regardless of what she wants, change is a comin', along with the grisly murder of one of the village's most beloved, mayhem between the villagers and the urbanites of Tri-City, and new dynamics of family dysfunction.

Get ready for a roller coaster ride from the peaks of new life, yummy food, and blossoming relationships to the valleys of slayings, chaos, and war. The residents of Leavensport are in for the battle of their lives, and it's up to Jolie, Ava, and their crew to determine the future of their village.

Welcome to Leavensport, Ohio, where *DEATH* takes a *DELICIOUS* turn!

Read on for a Sneak Peek at Chapter One of Punkin Strudel Mayhem which comes out October 29, 2021.

Chapter One

October in Leavensport was similar to Salem, Massachusetts in that our villagers LOVED to decorate and pay tribute to the witches, goblins, and spirits of the dead—a tad overkill if anyone asked me—but no one ever did. Don't get me wrong, I love a witch's costume as much as the next gal, but when Grandma Opal, my mom, and Aunt Fern dress up as the witches from Macbeth to recite the famous "Double, double, toil and trouble," incantation every single year since I can remember—well, let's just say I've come to despise it at times.

This year was no different. Actually, it was worse. The twin monsters I'm carrying around in my stomach were ready to pop out any day now and that day couldn't come soon enough. Ava and Delilah were only carrying one each inside them and they were both getting grumpier with each passing day. The Ohio sky matched my mood—misty, gray, and rumbling, threatening to cry all over the villagers of Leavensport. My mood swings had been out of control the last week and my vivid dreams had turned to nightmares. The doctor assured me this is normal for a woman carrying twins. Actually, I believe she said, "especially those due around the witching hour."

Again, I didn't see the humor in that.

Today, I could tell it was going to be *one of those days*. I woke to a drip falling on my face. Our new roof had sprung a leak and that seepage happened to be right over the spot where I laid my head to rest. After placing a large bucket where my pillow should be, I texted Mick to let him know, and, being the best husband in the world, he promised to meet the roofers this afternoon. I forced myself to not start the day in a bad mood and began humming "Monster Mash" as I went to the bathroom to brush my teeth. Bobbi Jo, our bobtail kitty, jumped up on the counter as I grabbed my toothbrush and butted her cute little calico head into my hand, launching my toothbrush into the toilet. I may have used some...unladylike...words momentarily, but I chalked it up as—well, like I said, *one of those days*. Rather than go to work with bad breath and gritty teeth, I opted to use my finger to at least freshen my mouth up a bit and used three times the amount of mouthwash than I usually did. Next, the hot water cut out halfway through my shower while the shampoo was bubbled up on my curly mop. The twins weren't thrilled with me for squealing as I the freezing water gushed over my head and body. They began kicking in protest.

The rest of the morning—at least getting ready to leave the house—went smoothly. Driving to work, I opted to play some relaxing, meditative music I'd found to help calm my anxiety for the last several months. I did as my YouTube videos instructed and took deep breaths, visualizing embracing the good and releasing the bad.

I felt my body begin to relax more as the twins settled down as I neared the center of the village, looking around at people out in the sprinkling rain, putting up cobwebbed decorations with large spiders in the center, witch's hats, cauldrons with green gunk that looked to be bubbling over at the side of the streets—OH CRAP! I was supposed to tell Grandma Opal to dig out our cast-iron cauldrons from her basement to use around the restaurant.

I clicked the button to call in the Honda CR-V. "Call Grandma," I said.

"Calling Ava," my robotic car ghost spoke back.

"What?" I cut it off. "CALL GRAND-MA!" I screamed at her then took a breath.

"Calling—" she started before I screeched the breaks and felt the seat belt cut into my chest— "Ava."

"What on Earth?" I looked behind me, then put my flashers on and got out of the car.

Three black kittens sat in the middle of the road, staring up at me, mewing. They looked exactly like Ava's three babies, Luna, Lily, and Lulu. Mick and I already had four cats of our own at home. We were both...well...*cat whipped*, to the say the least.

"Hi babies—are you Lily, Luna, and Lulu?" I asked.

The tiniest of the crew with a tiny white mark on her neck that looked like Ava's little Lily came right up to me as I bent down to pick her up. She purred loudly, leaning into my chest.

"Oooooo," I moaned.

Someone honked behind me and I glared at them and turned to make sure the other two didn't take off. They had moved to my feet nearly climbing my maternity dress.

"Move it!" Asher, who worked for Jackson Nestle—a man I despised—yelled from his truck.

"Go around me, you jerk face!" I yelled at him, then grabbed the other two with my free hand and put them in the back in a box I had.

"Hello—Jolie—JOLIE!" I heard Ava yelling from the speaker as I pulled over to the side of the road.

"Are your three girls at home?" I asked.

"Of course they are! Where else would they be?" Ava grumped at me.

"I'm staring at them right now, Jolie," I heard Delilah grumble.

"Why?" Ava barked.

Boy, not a good day for those two either.

"Nothing, I'm going to be late. I have to run to Dr. Libby's office first. I gotta go. I'll tell you about it later," I said, looking behind me to make sure no one was coming before I pulled back onto the road.

One of the kittens had jumped out of the box onto my shoulder at the same time digging her claws into me and I screeched and jerked the wheel as a large red blur ran into the Honda.

About the Author

Moving into her second decade working in education, Jodi Rath has decided to begin a life of crime in her The Cast Iron Skillet Mystery Series. Her passion for both mysteries and education led her to combine the two to create her own business, called MYS ED, where she splits her time between working as an adjunct for Ohio teachers and creating mischief in her fictional writing. She currently resides in a small, cozy village in Ohio with her husband and her nine cats.

Other Books by this Author

Links So We Can Stay Connected

Be sure to sign up for a monthly newsletter to get MORE of the Leavensport gang with free flash fiction, short stories, two-minute mysteries, cast-iron recipes, tips, and more. Subscribe to our monthly newsletter for a FREE Mystery A Month at http://eepurl.com/dIfXdb

Follow me on Facebook at https://www.facebook.com/authorjodirath

@jodirath is where you can find me on Twitter

www.jodirath.com

Upcoming Releases

Coming October 29, 2021, *Punkin Strudel Mayhem*

Look for a brand-new cozy series from Jodi Rath coming in 2023!